WHEN THE SKY BEGAN TO ROAR

ALICE BACH

WHEN THE SKY BEGAN TO ROAR

HOUGHTON MIFFLIN COMPANY   BOSTON   1984

Library of Congress Cataloging in Publication Data

Bach, Alice.
  When the sky began to roar.

  Summary: A tightly knit group of bright teenagers in
New York City indulge in vandalism and random acts of
violence for the thrill of it.
  I. Title
PZ7.B1314Wh 1984   [Fic]   84–12901
ISBN 0–395–36071–4

Printed in the United States of America

Q 10 9 8 7 6 5 4 3 2 1

For Judy Buck and Shirley Hawkinson,
my sisters for the long haul

There was a man of double deed
Sowed his garden full of seed.
When the seed began to grow,
'Twas like a garden full of snow;
When the snow began to melt,
'Twas like a ship without a belt;
When the ship began to sail,
'Twas like a bird without a tail;
When the bird began to fly,
'Twas like an eagle in the sky;
When the sky began to roar,
'Twas like a lion at the door;
When the door began to crack,
'Twas like a stick across my back;
When my back began to smart,
'Twas like a penknife in my heart;
When my heart began to bleed,
'Twas death and death and death indeed.

— *Old Nursery Rhyme*

Subway Heartbreak

New York October 15, (AP) — A teenage girl fell to her death early last evening from the subway platform of the Broadway IRT 96th Street station. Eyewitnesses said the girl had been standing with three youths just before the tragedy. The boys were not at the scene when the police arrived.

The medical examiner told reporters at the scene that death had been instantaneous with the impact of the train. Her identity has not been released, pending notification of next of kin.

"We're not ruling out that this young lady may have been a member of one of the teen cults that flourish in the city," said police spokesman Sergeant Maximo Alliandre. "We got files an inch thick on some of these weirdoes."

Police are asking anyone with information about the girl, or the three boys who were at the scene at the time of the tragedy, to contact them through special police hotline 988-2640. At present, the death is being called a suspicious suicide, pending the coroner's report.

WHEN THE SKY BEGAN TO ROAR

1

It was that sweaty kind of September afternoon when the glare from the sidewalks seemed hotter than the buttery sun melting over the Hudson River. There was no breeze in Riverside Park, but the grass under the trees was cool on their backs. The torrid day had one comfort. The four of them were home from vacations inflicted upon them by their parents. Vacations kept them apart.

"Why don't we go claim your apartment, *our* apartment, Peter?" Crunch Maxwell suggested, shielding his eyes from the rays of sun coming through the trees.

Wendy wiped her face with a white linen handkerchief. "This better not be a hoax."

All summer Peter Zeiss had been trekking around Taos with his parents, killing time until he could be one of the four again. He stood up quickly and brushed the grass from his jeans. "It's real, Wendy my girl. Lenore and Benny are staying in Taos until Benny attains enlightenment. The apartment is ours, all seven rooms, river view."

As they strode hip to hip through the dark lobby of

the building on Riverside Drive, Peter let out a joyous shriek. Its echo sounded ghostly in the deserted lobby. Wendy looked like whipped cream to him in spite of the ninety-degree heat. He turned the key in the lock and kissed the top of Wendy's head.

"What the hell was that for?" Elizabeth frowned and turned her back to them.

"One for you too, share and share alike," Peter engulfed her. Elizabeth smelled slightly gamey, wearing her usual sweatshirt and jeans. Her skin had a dingy look year-round. Peter knew once he had been back a few days he would not notice how Elizabeth looked.

Peter ran through the house flicking on air conditioners. The four didn't think along conventional tracks, which girl is cutest, which boy is hip or cool. They had passed all such teen topics without a word probably sometime back in fifth grade. They avoided idiot traps like the Video Arcade. None of them had seen a *Star Wars* movie.

They sat around the kitchen table, Crunch rolling a couple of joints, Elizabeth brewing a pot of Mexican coffee. Wendy opened a box of petit fours and put them in the center of the table. She shook her hair until it fell down her back, and reached for a cigarette. What a lady, Peter thought.

Elizabeth poured the coffee and began counting off a verbal list on her fingers.

Peter was missing the conversation. "What did you say, Lizard?"

"I said Demaret is merely where we go to school. We can't repeat last spring's crap. I can't believe we wasted time over that May Queen nonsense. I had to charm peo-

2

ple I haven't spoken to since general science so that Wendy could be crowned Queen of the May, *tra-la*." Elizabeth grabbed a petit four and popped it into Wendy's protesting mouth. "OK, you were a dazzling queen and it was swell seeing you so sparkly in your tin crown."

Peter understood what Elizabeth was leading up to, and beat her to the punch. "What Lizard is trying to say is that she wants no part of the Junior Mural. I don't agree."

"Batting a thousand, first day of regulation play!" Crunch said around a mouthful of chocolate cake. "Be reasonable, Lizzy. We are the best artists, we have an obligation."

"We swore last spring that Stonehenge would not get involved with those teen angels we go to school with," Elizabeth repeated. They'd called themselves Stonehenge, for the inscrutable megalithic stones in England, after Elizabeth had visited them one summer.

"Aside from the fact that I was the first May Queen who could *spell* May Queen, Crunch is right. We must do their silly mural, to prevent it from being totally bush league. Not *with* the class, Elizabeth, *for* the class." Wendy winked at Crunch. "We're going to splatter our brains all over the second floor in Technicolor."

"Artistically, of course," crowed Crunch. "In flawless taste."

"Those zombies won't know what hit 'em," Peter gloated.

Elizabeth hadn't expected to win. The mural was too tempting. To leave their mark on the walls of Demaret. Knowing she'd be shot down on the mural issue, she had a tidbit in reserve. "There's a new kid in our class, sup-

3

posed to be a math genius," she said, her eyebrows arched.

"A new kid? In our class?" Peter didn't care about the kid. He wanted to keep them talking. He hoped they'd stay late. He wasn't ready to face the apartment alone.

"They've arranged for him to take my father's intro astro lab. We'll find out what he's made of after Sam's told him the sun's only a second-rate star."

"Must be damn smart for Columbia to let him audit Professor Sam Goldman's class." Crunch looked at Peter. "We'd better check him out."

Peter reached for a pack of matches and lit another cigarette. "Even if he's in that lab I suspect he's a second-rate star." Peter passed the joint to Elizabeth. "Funny starting Demaret as a junior."

Wendy leered melodramatically into Peter's sour face. "Maybe he was bounced, maybe for something *extraordinary!*"

"They don't bounce geniuses, they cajole geniuses," Crunch said quickly. "Remember when Peter was new? In third grade? Hands in his pockets all day? *Wheeoo!*"

"And Lenore as class mother." Wendy said. "Those hideous cupcakes with tofu frosting." She peeled a pear and sliced it, then placed it on a plate with some Brie. Then she traced Peter's ear with her fingertip. He's ripe as the pear and has as much backbone as the Brie, she decided. She observed him a moment longer and then leaned over and blew softly on his suntanned cheek. "We'd never have become Stonehenge without Peter."

Elizabeth groaned as the others knew she would. "We've got to cancel calling ourselves Stonehenge. It's too

4

self-conscious." She glanced around the table for confirmation. "I know I started it, but I was in sixth grade, overly impressed with symbols."

"I guess the joke is a bit stale," said Wendy.

"Agree," Peter said instantly.

"No more Stonehenge? Decided and finished off so fast." Crunch pretended to weep. "You guys forgot to take your mercy pills this morning."

Peter licked a pink frosted cake. "Thanks for this celebration. Can you believe I survived eight weeks of tacos and cornmeal? Lenore, as I'm sure you've guessed, is now mega-squaw."

"She's already been a Hindu, a cabalist, a vegan, a whale lover, and a no-nuke. Doesn't leave her a whole lot of room," Elizabeth said. She was astonished at how completely all signs of Peter's parents had vanished from the apartment, even the acrid fragrance of the incense Lenore burned continually in shallow copper bowls had evaporated. Now with all her mess packed away, it was easier to believe she'd really left town. Gone were her hookah with the green glass bowl, the windchimes made from mother-of-pearl plastic discs, the chunky raw-clay primitive animals, dolls made from cornhusks, a mandala supposedly decorated by a Tibetan monk . . . all of it packed up and shipped to Taos.

The apartment seemed brooding and sullen without Lenore's jubilation. Elizabeth had secretly cheered for Lenore; her looney embrace of every craze that hit the Upper West Side of New York was touching. Elizabeth recognized her own need to be surrounded by stacks of

5

unread books as her protection against the world, though living in her mother's house had rescued Elizabeth from blatantly collecting props the way Lenore did.

Her mother, Tess, would scoff at heralding one's love of music by wearing a Beethoven sweatshirt as Lenore did. Tess would no more think of disguising a worn seat cushion with an afghan (one of Lenore's standard decorating tricks) than she would hang her underwear to dry on the living room mantelpiece.

"What's their house like, Peter?" Elizabeth asked.

"So far it's no-frills adobe, but before I left, Lenore was scheming to trade down to a hut. 'I want to cook over an open fire, Benny; we can smoke peyote in clay pipes, Benny!'" Peter whined in accurate imitation of his mother.

"Ma and Pa Native America," Crunch slapped Peter on the back. "You're well out of it, my boy."

In June, Peter had assumed the Taos adventure would hang heavy on Lenore by August. They'd be home and their tans faded before school opened. He wondered why she didn't see how predictable and transparent she was. Her whole desire to drag them to Taos was nothing but a ruse to keep Benny away from his models, especially the one she'd caught him with, Ribbon Candy.

"Scummy little coward, getting it on with that anorectic chick; a man's no better than his fantasies." Lenore had snapped several sticks of bamboo from Peter's window-shade while she raged.

"Someone said that a mother's greatest contribution to the women's movement is her sons. Believe me, you're not

6

going to be crippled by neurotic bonds. No shrink's going to lay that trip on me." In spite of the passion in her voice, Peter assessed the damage at a month, six weeks tops. Every summer he ended up as the focal point of one of Lenore's visions — a working dairy farm, a children's traveling orchestra, a computer camp. Last summer he'd almost drowned shooting the Snake River rapids.

"We want a house exactly like Georgia O'Keeffe's," Lenore told the real estate agent. Luckily the first house suited her. "In earth only can we grow," Lenore explained to her son, while smearing some dirt on the backs of his hands.

"We all need cleansing," murmured Benny, a note of resignation in his voice.

"Why did you have to get caught?" Peter asked him while Lenore was cutting a deal with the agent. Stonehenge never gets caught, Peter added silently, not lifting the punch bowl from Tiffany's, not disguising the statue of Colonel Armand in Central Park as Donald Duck. We haven't paid for a subway ride in months. Yet I get stuck, sentenced to a summer in solitary, utterly unfair. Don't drag me into your games with Benny, Lenore. He waited 'til Benny's attention had been caught by a chief's headdress to slip a couple of pipes into his jeans pocket.

Peter's hatred of the house increased. Whitewashed clay, it reminded him of a discarded flowerpot. What would anyone want with this parched uneven earth, studded with stones bleached white as the sky? In New York the dense air would smell of dog shit and rotting garbage. One could reconstruct a city of people from the overflowing garbage cans along one block of Upper Broadway.

7

The weeks turned into a month, and Benny was negotiating new alliances with Lenore. He reacted like a six-foot banana on *Let's Make a Deal* when a neighbor offered to sell them her foot-pedaled potter's wheel. He raved about the morning light reflected off the mountains. It slowly dawned on Peter that he might be going back to New York alone.

Benny avoided his questions. "New York's finished for me and Lenore," he mumbled, unable to meet Peter's angry gaze.

"You have no right." Peter's eyes were dilated with rage. "*I'm* supposed to be the kid."

Back in the New York apartment, Lenore seemed to be in every room when Peter entered it. "Remember Lutie cleans Mondays and Wednesdays. Leave your laundry where she can find it. Granma and Pop-pop are just downstairs, three flights; it's not as though you'll be alone. How I wish I could be selfish and keep you here with me! We could get a couple of horses and ride into the hills. But a mother must let go. You know what happens to boys whose mothers won't let them go? They become *macho*. It's an instinct you have to fight — being a mother. Not every woman's as tough as I am. Remember how my heart broke when Andy went off to Sri Lanka? If I hadn't fought Benny, my Andy'd be peering at some computer screen at MIT missing this peak experience."

Her voice followed Peter through the airport and onto the plane. "Benny's going to take pictures of the chief. We'll send you prints." Peter suspected Andy's insistence on living in Sri Lanka was motivated more by a need to block out that voice than by some spiritual razzle. Smart boy, my brother, Peter thought, as the plane flew across the Mississippi. If I didn't have Stonehenge, I'd catch the next flight to a peak experience too.

The scent of Wendy's perfume brought him back to the present. She was really electric today. "We've got a club-house, just like Andy Hardy," she crooned, her skin glow-ing. Dancing around them, she embraced the hat rack and rubbed her cheek against the kitchen wall.

"Don't get too attached to this place," Peter warned her. "A steady diet of Lenore caroling Castaneda around the cactus and Benny'll be begging for a glimpse of the IRT."

Crunch ran his finger over the gritty window ledge. "We don't need them. Not sure we ever did. Except for the obvious feeding and diapering business."

"Which most of us have outgrown," Wendy said, her mood cooling quickly.

The gift of tongues, they've all got it, Elizabeth thought.

"Guess who ripped off Lenore's stash?" Peter ran into his bedroom and returned a few moments later. "First-class Mexicali rose."

They exchanged grins, each one a piece of the other's smile.

Vinnie Santini lay on his back. Three in the morning. He was probably the only human being awake on Staten Is-land. He frowned at his new digital clock. Five more hours until he'd be trapped in that snotty school of rich kids, none of whom he'd ever met, in a building he'd never seen.

Another hour clicked by on his snazzy clock. Vinnie knew the clock represented some fuzzy notion Pop had about split-second accuracy in that foreign world, Manhattan, that the Santinis knew only from watching the local TV news. Ma rousing him before she went to Mass was no longer good enough. If only he'd had the guts when they'd bought him the clothes and the clock to insist he didn't need fancy equipment; Manhattan's in the same time zone.

He heard Ma and Pop's bed creak. A few minutes later Ma was banging the metal lid of the milk box. The kettle clanged on the stove. "I'm ready, Ma," his sister-in-law Patsy yelled through the wall from her kitchen next door. Vinnie watched his mother from the stairs. He felt reassured by the familiar *slap slap slap* of her carpet slippers. She bent to put on her shoes, squat black shoes, nicked white on the inside of the heels from rubbing one shoe against the other when she walked. "You up, Sal?" she hollered as she tied her purple scarf under her chin.

"Vinnie! Off the stairs and brush you teeth." She didn't pause to look at him. "Use that mouthwash I got."

"Piccolino, what you doin' on the steps?" Pop stood over him fastening the suspenders of his painter's overalls. "Get in the shower! Now!"

"I took one last night."

"And soap good down there, you know."

Standing under the hot water, Vinnie cursed Father Loggia for selling them a bill of goods about Demaret.

"What you sayin'?" Berto punched his arm through the shower curtain.

"Hand me a towel." Vinnie dried himself and stepped into his undershorts. Had Berto always sat on the john seat watching him dress? "Get something to do, Berto, and stop pulling the paper off the roller."

Berto was not playing with a full deck. Sister Margaret Mary said he couldn't learn same as other boys, so they didn't promote him to the fifth grade. Which made Vinnie's smarts all the more miraculous. No way he could've talked them out of this school across the bay.

Vinnie admired the fit of his sport jacket and new ten-dollar shirt. "Look out, here comes Robert de Niro. Hey, Ma!"

At breakfast, Pop blessed himself and looked up. "Mama, should he take an extra shirt in case he sweats?"

"You wash good, Vinnie?"

"Yes, Ma." He glanced at his father, but the old man was too cagey to give away how he felt about this school business. If Father Loggia said it was a good idea, that was enough for the Santinis.

"Father Loggia better total up a lot of points for delivering me to Demaret."

"You not too special for a smack, talkin' against the priest." Ma spit on her finger and rubbed at a fleck of egg on Vinnie's cheek. "Kiss Mama goodbye."

Vinnie had known they were definitely sending him to this preppie palace the night of Pop's birthday dinner. Father Loggia rose to give the blessing. It was a particularly flowery prayer, ending with a tremulous plea to the Blessed Virgin.

". . . and we ask that young Vincent may be given the opportunity to use the gifts our Heavenly Father has so graciously given him. We ask You to intercede with Your Son for a full scholarship to Demaret School."

The old snake! Vinnie squeezed his eyes together.

Ma pulled her rosary from the pocket of her dress. *Hail Mary, full of grace* . . . That's it, sighed Vinnie, two years in the death house learning what rich kids learn. He'd memorized the brochure extolling Demaret:

"The Demaret School is three turn-of-the-century brownstones connected by smoked-glass tunnels. Designed by Oskar Vilholt, the award-winning structure blends with the Victorian houses on this tree-lined street in one of New York's most fashionable neighborhoods . . .

"Demaret is respectful of the past, but we value both our traditions and our right to be different; to require disciplined behavior, yet to be mindful of the individual student's differences. We teach the significant rather than the trendy; we reward excellence in all its guises."

On the early-morning ferry a strong breeze off the water caused Vincent to shiver. Get your scholarship boy's ass in gear. Down the ramp and onto the subway. Trip is longer than I thought, can't be late, they want their scholarship boy there in plenty of time to learn how to get rich. That's how they reward scholarly excellence! Sure, and pigs fly south for the winter.

Holy Mother of God! Through his confusion, voices throbbed and colors flickered. Every inch of wall space in the entrance hall was covered with murals. Rich kids' graffiti. I'd like to meet the guy who cartoons this good, he thought, his cautiousness dissolving into admiration.

12

What ideas! He leaned against a wall of lockers and studied the caricatures. All the Peanuts gang were piled into a red jeep: the Ayatollah sat on the hood of a Batmobile chatting with Tricky Dick Nixon. A scrawled caption read: Would you buy a used car from these men?

Vinnie moved toward the center stairs. Sure was noisier without nuns patrolling the halls. He wished someone would talk to him, but no one did. He didn't want to make the wrong moves. A bell rang. The students rushed up the stairs. "How do I get to the principal's office?" Vinnie asked a tall lean boy in paint-spattered jeans. He was eating corn chips by the handful.

"See over there, where the mural becomes blue with white clouds — well, follow it 'til you come to the Pearly Gates."

Gold-plated bastard, Vinnie muttered as he stamped down the hall. He came to a door, looked up, and laughed out loud. The Supremes were playing gold harps in front of an immense papier-mâché structure.

"All *right!*" he cried. He was indeed before the Pearly Gates. Painted just the way Vinnie would have done it — lurid silver with gold-leaf lettering. Zippety-do-da zippety-a!

For two weeks Vinnie sat at lunch alone, pretending to study. He was watching a girl who seemed to have been dipped in gold. Her hair lay on her shoulders in thick coils. She'd caught him looking, gave him a slit-eyed smile. He had no idea about the Demaret routine with girls. The ones he had always known were kids he'd taken catechism with, girls from the neighborhood. He hadn't a clue about the golden girl. Wendy was her name, but he was sure she'd cost him more than the chem book and history text combined.

One morning in early October Vinnie arrived half an hour late. The subway had sat outside the 34th Street station for almost forty minutes. Flinging open the school door, Vinnie collided with the Pearly Gates boy, scattering his bag of corn chips. Vinnie dropped his books on the floor and attempted to pick up the chips, thinking this guy must be a weirdo deluxe.

"Crunch Maxwell, junior, Mr. Giddon's homeroom."

"Vinnie Santini, junior, Miss Rogers."

"You're the new one." He glanced at his watch. "You need a late pass."

"Left my house at six-thirty, the bloody train was stalled, give the bad marks to the transit system, buddy."

"Suck my toe, I got told cold."

"I didn't mean to come on so heavy," Vinnie muttered.

Crunch had gray eyes and light brown hair, shiny as a girl's. Very white even teeth. He tossed his head frequently and combed his fingers through his hair. In this light it had a silver cast to it. He stood easily, a guy really comfortable in his body, so casual he might have been leaning up against an invisible wall. Vinnie decided to take a chance.

"Got my ass in a sling this morning."

"Carrying a load that heavy you make Quasimodo look like Posture Pete." Crunch held out his bag of corn chips. "Have a crunch?"

"Thanks."

Crunch tossed his head, raked his hair, and grimaced.

14

"We've all been hangin' out so long, we turn to stone around strangers. Was it like that at your old school, Beppo? I've got this habit — I make up names for people I like. Mind if I call you Beppo?"

Vinnie shrugged, tucked his thumbs in his pants pockets.

"OK, *Beppo*. Here's your pass for class. We start the mural on the second-floor corridor next week. Demaret tradition for juniors. A few of us are getting together after seventh period today. You interested?"

"Sounds good."

"Wendy Tippett is chairman. She's got Miss Rogers too. Blond, curly hair —"

"I know who she is. She's an artist?"

"The best. Won last year's city competition. Also she was May Queen. You ever win any competitions?"

"Science fairs."

"Mural's unveiled on Halloween, so we don't have much time. Wendy has a packet of sketches. Her ideas are dynamite. You'll see."

"What about your ideas?"

"Wendy's ideas suit me." Crunch stuffed his chips into his backpack. Vinnie understood that he was ending the conversation.

"Tell you what, Beppo. There's a tall girl in your seventh-period calculus class, Elizabeth Goldman."

Beppo nodded. When he first saw her, he'd thought she looked like she'd been embalmed at a discount. Elizabeth secured her braid on top of her head as though she wanted to forget she had hair.

"You tell her I said you should come with her."

15

Beppo walked to class, amazed it had been so easy.

He felt as new as his name, as though Crunch had pressed his fingers deep into Vinnie's soft bones and left the correct answers there, the genes for how to be cool. Crunch was a wizard. Unlike Vinnie's former friends at St. Anne's, Crunch hadn't grown up cowed by the threat of Purgatory. Wendy! He leaned over her shoulder after school while she was sketching cartoons for the mural and inhaled her fragrant hair. Wendy had never looked at him, never addressed a word to him. But he was hooked.

The morning after the meeting, Crunch and his friends stopped at Vinnie's locker. "Told you guys this Beppo had something special. Let's bring him with us to the next meeting. That is, if you *want* to support our sketches, you are voting with us, Beppo?"

By the Halloween party Vincent Santini had become Beppo to the whole school, the brilliant kid who pulled down heavy science awards and could cartoon like a pro. Girls tinkled around him during lunch, guys swatted his ass in the halls. But Crunch and his friends had cooled toward him after the mural was finished.

A few weeks later Vinnie arrived at chem behind Elizabeth. The door to the classroom was covered with cork squares. Wendy and Peter grinned as Elizabeth gasped in delight. A ruffled dotted-swiss heart was tacked to the cork, and printed in ornate Gothic letters on its red-satin center were the words "Elizabeth Goldman loves Marcel Proust."

Crunch kissed her. "It's your day, darlin'."

"Happy Birthday, Elizabeth," Vinnie said primly, vowing to find out who Marcel Proust was. He wished he knew how to tell them he could have thought up the heart business. All he wanted was a chance.

ABC Eyewitness News, "*The Eleven O'Clock Report*"

"We have in the studio with us the motorman who was driving the tragic train that spelled death this evening for an unidentified teenage girl. Mr. Emerson, how did the accident happen?"

"I been motorman on the Broadway line more than eight years, and before that I was on the Brighton Beach line, and never, never, did I see a jumper before tonight. Well you live long enough you see everything in this city. They say there used to be more jumpers back in the thirties, one or two jumped nearly every month, but that was usually the Canarsie Run. They don't jump in Manhattan."

"You say jump. Has it been ruled a suicide then?"

"What else? Somebody push a nice young girl, got her whole life ahead of her? Not in Manhattan. But I don't know for sure, you see. Don't quote me it's a jumper."

"What safety precautions does the MTA take in cases like this? After all, we all ride the trains every day!"

"Wasn't nothing for us to do. Tunnel was clear, we got the green light, by the time I see this flash, we couldn't have stopped, no matter what. Didn't know it was a jumper 'til after it happen and us halfway down the track. You can't see down on the track when you up high in the cab."

"What about the brakes?"

"Stopped, didn't we! Mostly the cars is good, but with so many mechanics laid off 'cause of the cutbacks, well, you know. Thank Mr. Mayor for that. I'm not saying we could've stopped, we didn't see nothin' to stop for, you see . . ."

2

It was Saturday afternoon; a dull gray late November sky matched their mood. No one could think of a caper worth leaving the apartment for. Wendy had suggested a challenging rip-off: getting a painting off the wall of a Soho art gallery. But no one wanted to go so far downtown. Peter thought they should go to a pizza place and pretend to be foreign kids who didn't speak English. But they'd run that caper in sixth grade.

"Why don't we give Beppo a chance. Bet he'd have new ideas for capers. We need new blood," Crunch said.

"Demaret gives scholarships; we don't," Wendy tossed her hair over her shoulder and dipped a sugar cube in her cup of espresso. Then she put her lips around the cube and slowly sucked the coffee from it. Crunch's roving eye was going to get them in trouble one day — always picking up strays, dropping them at her feet for approval.

Peter hastily looked away. Lately everything Wendy did turned him on. "One good thing about Beppo is that we'd always know where to find him. He's roofed in the computer room, with all those scuzzy hackers."

Elizabeth wanted to be fair to Beppo. The way he stammered around the Goldmans' living room as though he were there to repair a window sash touched her. "He did brilliant work on the mural, and my father thinks —"

"Who cares what your father thinks," Crunch snapped. "We don't live by their rules."

"I'm on your side," Elizabeth glowered at Crunch. "No need to be such a prune."

"Maybe the Italian could fit it," Peter said cautiously, "if we can break his arcade habit. Heard him bragging to some kid about his score."

"That's what I mean," said Wendy, leaning across the table. "He's trendy. Probably aspires to the *Guinness Book of World Records*."

Crunch waved aside her objections. "He'll dump that crap if we let him hang out with us now and then. He doesn't know any better. Trust me."

Wendy went to the window and looked down at the river scene. Few people were jogging against the bitter wind. Wendy loathed aging joggers, buffoons puffing along the path hoping to outrun their sloppy lives. Vinnie wasn't a bad choice. He was taller and leaner than most Italians. He had a tempting smile, teeth white as ice. Probably been screwing since he was ten. Peter and Crunch were as green as she was. It would take them years to pick up what Santini already knew. Not a bad choice at all. Forgive me Father for banishing Your Church from Beppo's scholarship mind. I shall leadeth him by the still Hudson, I shall make him lie down. My will be done.

Wendy had been in mortal combat with the Lord ever since she could remember. Not the compliant God who smiled benevolently on her father's business investments, but the God who crackled through her dreams, overhearing her most wicked thoughts. Joining the Catholic Church, an act that drove her father into a silent rage that lasted for weeks, she'd tried to prove to Curtis there was a power greater than his. At first she believed it too. Confessions poured out of her, some of them even true. But none of the priests was as clever as her father. Wendy could trip them up without effort.

Beppo was one of the Catholics the Church loved. Brought up to believe obedience to the Church was the ticket to everlasting rewards in this world and the next. But Wendy had detected in his hungry eyes that he was ready to bolt, he was set to throw off the comfort of the Blessed Madonna. *My will be done.*

Wendy glanced over her shoulder. Peter was opening the envelope of Benny's weekly packet of photos. Santini'd never understand how Lenore and Benny could hang out in Taos, allowing their son to go it alone in New York. Santini probably figured on living with his mama 'til they laid her out.

Reluctantly, Wendy returned to the table. "Another Kodacolor extravaganza by Benny Zeiss on loan to the Infinite."

Sometimes you're a prize bitch, Elizabeth wanted to say.

"Benny's doing terrific work. Maybe this time Lenore was right. Taos does seem to suit Benny's style," Peter said, wishing he could stop defending his parents.

"And we are suited to this apartment," Crunch reminded him.

"They're bound to come back by New Year's, even if

Benny has copyrighted the stunning mesa at sunset,"
Elizabeth said, holding up one of the photographs.
"Lenore will need another shot of motherhood. Just wait
and see."

Wendy loathed the wisps of hair straggling out of
Elizabeth's braid. It was no act. Elizabeth didn't care.
She washed her hair begrudgingly. She changed her out-
fit solely so that the clothes could be laundered. She
stared unseeing into shop windows and skipped the makeup ads in magazines. "Remember in third or fourth
grade, must have been fourth because Peter was with us,
Tess kept taking pictures during your birthday party?"
Wendy asked slyly.

Elizabeth's stomach lurched. "And they were all of
you." She clenched her sweating hands in her lap.
"You've told that story so often it has the patina of
myth."

Wendy fidgeted with a pack of rolling papers. She
should never underestimate Elizabeth. It wasn't solely her
astronomical IQ. There was a stubbornness at her core;
she couldn't be bullied as easily as the boys could.

"Anyway Miss Pure and White, why don't you wear
black for a week, and raunchy unironed shirts, to break
you of that mania for two baths a day?"

"The day you ask Tess to spend Saturday shopping
with you," Wendy said, drawing in a lungful of smoke
and blowing several perfect smoke rings. "To break your
mania for shabbiness."

Peter moved closer to Wendy so she would remember
he was on her side. "Dynamite, Wendy," his voice had
erupted out of him, graceless as a belch.

"Anyway, I look marvelous in black." Wendy never took her eyes from Elizabeth's face.

Crunch jumped to his feet. "Psych games, *wheeoo!*" He sat down quickly, seeing that neither Wendy nor Elizabeth had a vestige of anger on her face. Surprisingly they were smiling at each other. Peter had been tracking the wrong scent, and Crunch had nearly stumbled into the hole after him. He sat down and cleared his face of all expression.

"Nobody knows us as well as we understand each other," Elizabeth said. "More and more we are one. Mother and father. Star and astronomer. Whatever we demand from each other is right."

"We are one," repeated Peter.

Wendy stared unblinkingly. "We can devise our own penance too," she said.

Crunch stretched out on the floor and balanced a can of Coke on his chest. "You rerunning Mother Church, Wendy? Come on, confess!"

"Don't be a jackass. If there's one thing I learned during my stint in the Church it's that their tragic flaw is giving penance equally, same as the Host. One wafer, one tongue, world without end. Some of those priests have the IQ of gnats, which explains why they can't distinguish between their sins and mine."

"Priests' sins are a lot duller than ours," Crunch said, growing bored with the turn the conversation was taking.

Wendy tweaked the toe of Crunch's sneaker. "We are the only ones who can weigh what we do."

"Wendy's right," said Elizabeth. "We can examine our own failings, and correct the course."

Crunch was impressed. How many people ever saw the old tried and true as clearly as they did. "No doubt about it, we're the whole enchilada."

"If each person admits when he's screwed up, and decides his own punishment, we can keep control of our lives." Peter pushed his hair off his forehead. "We don't need any outsider telling us what should be."

"OK, we need specifics. How long do we give the person and who judges if the penance is honest?" asked Wendy. "We can't get hung up on power." She was thinking of her father, laying down laws like a dictator in a banana republic. Shouting if dinner was delayed five minutes, criticizing everything from her mother's cream sauce to the Governor's veto of the death penalty. Curtis loved the death penalty.

Elizabeth's heart was hammering. Maybe they could create a perfect world for themselves. No one was more clever and no one could be closer than they were. "We should take turns being in charge, then no one will have to wrestle the power away from the *leader,* because the power will come their way every fourth week.

"Sounds like the ideal system. If one of us does something they know needs nipping in the bud, well, they decide on their own how to nip it, and report the result to the person in charge." Usually Elizabeth hoarded words like candy. Today she felt as pretty as Wendy and as nimble with words as Crunch. "And if we sense that one of us hasn't owned up to a flaw, well then, we talk to that person —"

"Not that we'll find a whole lot wrong with perfect old us," Crunch said, swallowing the remainder of his Coke.

24

They laughed and entwined their arms. "Excellent, excellent!"

For Peter the new rules were not enough. Sure it was exhilarating to know that they'd created an air-tight solution to the problem of admitting faults without committing treachery. But when all was said and done, they still went home every night, leaving him with the dark apartment, which had all the charm of a railway station after the last train of the night has whistled through.

Deciding to let Santini hang out with them now and then didn't matter much to Peter. Vinnie, or Beppo, or whatever they ended up naming him, would be on his way back to Staten Island every night before dark, if he wasn't hurrying to the arcade to better his Donkey Kong score. The others didn't seem to notice Peter's loneliness, and he certainly wasn't about to admit to them that he envied them their parents more than they envied him his freedom. Part of that freedom was the one secret he kept from them — he was getting it on with Crunch's younger sister, Gina, every Thursday night, regular as an orthodontist appointment.

It had begun the week he got back from Taos. He was still high on his freedom, still accepting congratulations as though he'd pulled off something unheard of. Gina had wandered over to the apartment one afternoon, carrying her rehearsal gear and ballet shoes in a Metropolitan Opera totebag. He had rolled her a joint. Giggling nervously, she dragged on it and begged him not to tell Crunch. Her brother would kill her if he caught her smoking dope.

They sat on opposite ends of the living room couch, talking politely about their summers. Looking at her lovely wide-eyed face, Peter decided she'd be terrific proof of his freedom. He pulled her onto his lap. Immediately he knew she'd work out, so warm and sweet, filling his arms, fitting herself against him. He kissed her a few times, but then she pulled away and flew around the living room, patting the chairs as though they were people.

Hugging a throw pillow to her chest, she tried to smile. But her gray eyes were wary, watching him. The price is patience, he told himself. "Sorry if I came on too strong, babe. But you've grown up this summer. That ballet camp has turned you into a very desirable girl."

It was true. Her long legs were tan and muscular. She moved with the innate grace of a dancer.

Peter looked at Gina solemnly. He felt as though he were offering hunks of bread to a pigeon. It took another couple of tries, but three days later, he had the pigeon. He bound her to him, calling her his love, claiming her every Thursday night after dance class. It was the only night she could get out of the house. That still left him empty every other night after his friends drifted home.

"Tess has another fund raiser tonight. Let's hang out at Peter's and order pizza," Elizabeth said in the cafeteria the following Monday. She had to speak more loudly than was comfortable for her because the noise in the cafeteria was deafening.

Crunch snatched her pencil from her hand. "Let's make a list of things we need. Better than pizza. How about wine, and some of that runny cheese Wendy loves."

26

Wendy grabbed Peter's hands and clapped them like cymbals. From a table two rows away Vinnie studied them. Wendy caught his eye and lifted her hand in salute.

Wendy noticed Vinnie's flushed discomfort and leaned toward the group. Stroking Peter's arm she said softly, "I've been thinking, Peter Pumpkin, you should give each of us a key to your castle." Santini was still watching.

"My grandmother might find out," Peter said uneasily.

"There's no special reason you want to keep us out?"

"Hiding ladies under the bed, Peter?"

"Not under the bed, Lizard. Behind the books in Benny's studio."

"I'd feel more equal if I had a key," Wendy said.

Peter crushed his milk carton in his right hand. "I don't have a key to your apartment."

"Who'd want one?" sighed Wendy. "I thought it would make us more like a family, each having a key to the house, you know."

"Agree," Crunch said quickly.

"Agree," Elizabeth said an instant later.

The key would deliver the death blow to Curtis's threats. No matter how many people saw him as Mr. Congeniality, Wendy knew he was no merry old soul. Last night he'd refused to let her use the telephone to call Elizabeth. "It's after nine. Any business you and your friends have to transact should take place before eight-thirty."

"Don't you think that's a bit arbitrary?" Wendy hadn't been paying much attention. She saw it more as a minor annoyance than a full-scale issue. So she was unprepared when her father threw his magazine across the floor and bellowed at her.

"Damn right it's arbitrary. This is my house and I call the shots. Anytime you decide it's too *arbitrary,* you can pack your bags and get out!"

Wendy glared at him, unmoving, an animal trapped in the headlights of an onrushing car. When her heart stopped pounding, she turned her back and fled the room. But he bore down on her and almost tore the door to her room off its hinges.

"Don't you walk away when I'm talking to you. Clean up this room!" He flung back the curtains and opened her window. "I don't give a damn if you kill yourself with cigarettes, but I will not have this place stinking of stale smoke. Your mother and I have to live too, you know. This is not your private retreat."

"I'll get out all right," she said evenly, her voice a low-pitched hiss, "just as soon as I can. You can depend on it."

"Don't threaten me. I'm not required to send you to college. As soon as you're eighteen, you're free to louse up your life any way you see fit, but it will not be with my bankroll."

Regarding himself for an instant in the long mirror behind Wendy's door, he cleared his throat and left the room.

The group concentrated on the food on their trays, each one uneasy at Wendy's angry squint. She was staring at the far wall of the cafeteria. Elizabeth glanced furtively in that direction but could see nothing that would have turned Wendy so pale.

Crunch tapped his milk carton. "Look, guys, I sort of

promised we'd listen to Santini's ideas for the Twelfth-night Party. Since we agreed to give him a chance —"

"I don't recall agreeing to an audition —" Wendy snapped.

"You didn't say no, Wendybird," Crunch hesitated. "Is it OK?"

Mollified, Wendy nodded and gestured to Vinnie to join them.

They're all looking me over, Vinnie thought, bowing his head low, his face almost in his lunch plate. Please God, don't let me blow it. Let me be cool.

Crunch clapped Vinnie on the back. "Bet you've got an f'ing brilliant idea, Beppo old bean."

Wendy moved over one seat so Vinnie could sit next to her. She flashed him a smile that stung like a whip. "Let's hear it, hotshot."

"See, I thought we could create our own laserium, hook up the computer to a light board, set up random sequences. No good, huh? OK, what about the inside of an alien ship? Very high-tech —" he glanced at Wendy.

"This is going to be more of a challenge than we thought," she said as though Vinnie'd been bleeped off the screen.

Vinnie tried desperately to save himself. "We could make our own game, you know a Demaret Kong, saving the golden-haired maiden." He looked at Wendy. But flat-footed flattery only made her colder. "What about using splashy color graphics, and kind of computer-sounding music as the kids are coming in." He'd bombed out of her universe, that much was plain.

Crunch crumpled the napkins on the table and shrugged, as though the TV had crapped out when they were all primed to watch a special show. "Quit while you're ahead, Pac-man."

"I like the laserium idea. With all those pulsing spinning lights, nobody will notice that none of us is there," Elizabeth said, winking at Vinnie.

"OK," Wendy sighed. "Peter can present it to the class this afternoon."

Elizabeth cleared her throat. "Beppo will present it," she said quietly.

"We're getting like old folks, every day the same routine. Let's spice it up, do something exciting in the New Year," Crunch said while they were waiting for Elizabeth to arrive at Peter's.

"You mean like scoring coke?" Peter said. It was only two weeks until Christmas, and Lenore's plans for the holidays sounded vague.

"Dope's impersonal. What about taking in a new member?" Crunch said.

"Wouldn't by any chance mean that microchip brain from Staten Island?" Wendy asked, but not harshly. Ever since the class went gung ho for Beppo's idea, she'd been expecting that they'd take him in. Crunch was reacting a week earlier than she'd figured he would. Silly of him not to have waited for Elizabeth to back him up.

"Why not take in a girl?" Peter was about to mention Gina when there was a knock on the door. He let Elizabeth in and asked her if she thought they needed new blood. He suggested Gina. Elizabeth looked startled and shook her head. "Don't mention that around Crunch. Gina's his private property. He'll crucify you." Peter cleared his face as they rejoined the group. Crunch was talking. "Don't forget, Wendybird, he's wiped clean as a dagger after a crime, perfect for us. He has nothing to un-learn," Crunch finished smoothly and turned to Elizabeth. "OK, Beppo, in?"

The opportunity to get them to accept Gina had flown. She'll have to remain on the back burner, Peter told him-self. Elizabeth's right. Crunch would explode if he sug-gested it. He couldn't bear to think what Crunch would do if he ever found out about Thursdays. He socked Crunch's arm. "Beppo is OK with me."

"Well he's not OK with me; he looks at me as though I'm fresh meat and he hasn't made a kill in weeks," Wendy snapped.

Crunch glared at her. "The closer he gets, the less he'll look."

Peter tried to breathe more softly.

"You know how I get," Wendy said slowly, catching each one's glance, "when I am pissed off. You didn't de-serve my crap, Crunch." He held his breath. It wasn't like her to embarrass them. "I was acting like my father, always insisting on the upper hand. We will still be tight, even with Santini. We'll be five as one. The new rules will bind us together, even with him." She leaned over the table and caressed the wood tenderly.

"Five as one," murmured Crunch. He made an effort to contain his joy. He wished they were all on the floor, tangled up like puppies. Peter stuffed his mouth with corn chips and shook the rest onto the table.

31

Crunch stood up and struck at an imaginary tennis ball with an imaginary racquet, swatting at the tension in the air. "Guess our Wendybird got the last word after all," he said, reaching over to field a ball from his backhand.

"Let's meet here tomorrow around eleven."

"What about school, dummie. It's *Friday*."

"I thought today was Friday," Peter said and smacked himself in the head. "One day's the same as the next. OK, can we tell Beppo tomorrow that he's in?"

"Nothing so formal, Peter. We'll tell him to come back with us after school, and gradually he'll see that he's in."

"What if Santini turns out to be soggy pasta, after all my negotiating in his behalf?" Crunch screwed up his face in disgust.

Wendy squeezed his shoulder. "We'll heat him up."

She's giving in now, but she'd going to want something in return, Crunch thought. He picked up a dishtowel from the sink and wiped his face.

Lying in bed that night, Peter's head was reeling. Wendy had been setting fires all afternoon. She's come back to his apartment after they'd all gone, on the pretext of having forgotten her copy of *King Lear*. He'd crawled under the couch because Wendy thought she'd dropped it near there. When he looked up, her face was a few inches from his. She had kissed him, her tongue stretching deep into his mouth. She'd run her hands along his inner thighs, slowly. Never saying a word, her eyes locked into his all the while.

What an afternoon! She'd never kissed him in that way before. Remembering her kiss made him desperately lonely. If only Gina could stay with him all night long. Someday Peter was going to slip, he could feel it, while he and Crunch were sharing a toke, that's when he'd bungle it — damn secret, making a mine field out of every conversation, damn secret that Crunch would never want to know. If only Peter had a sister for him.

Wendy's kiss had pulled the scab off Peter's heart. She was the dangerous one, the one who could turn his breath dry like dust in his mouth. Sweet Gina had been given to him; he would have to earn Wendy.

Overheard at Ruggio's Market:

"I'm standing on the platform waiting for the train. I don't notice anybody in particular. The station's crowded, the newsstand guy had just closed down and was locking his metal doors. I'm watching him when three boys come running down the steps, well, they're probably late teens, I keep my eye on 'em because you never know these days, anyway they push right through the exit door, don't even pretend to pay the fare."

"Those blasted kids; that's why the fare goes up every time you turn around. So go on, what happened then?"

"You're right. Bunch of hoods. And these ones were white, looked like neighborhood boys. Now I didn't see them actually say anything to the poor girl. It all happened so fast, then someone grabs me and pulls me away from the edge, screaming, "Oh my God. She's gone over. Don't look, don't look!" Don't have to tell me not to look. I don't have a stomach for this kind of tragedy. But I see one of the boys look over the edge and then he turns around and barfs, right on the platform. Probably high on drugs."

"Don't mind telling you, it scares me to death. These trains not being able to stop and all. What if you slip or one of these lousy punks bumps you, you got as much chance as a mosquito. MTA got to do something!"

"I can't think about it. I won't think about it."

34

3

I disappoint my mother." Elizabeth sighed and flopped into her chair next to Crunch. They were sitting around the oak table in the Zeisses' kitchen. To everyone's surprise Lenore and Benny had made a quick visit to New York for Christmas and scuttled back to the desert. "Even at Aunt Janet and Uncle Dicky's funeral last week, certainly a *family* occasion, Tess frowned at me, when she remembered that I was there at all."

Elizabeth did not add: I hate myself for dreading my cousin Kate. I hate myself for wishing her parents hadn't been smashed to bits last week in that dismal car accident solely because I don't want milk and honey Kate Callahan living in the next room.

Peter stood on his head, his body straight as a candle. To acknowledge the cheers of Wendy and Beppo, he shook out his pockets. Coins rang as they bounced off the bare floor. "Cheer up, Lizard. You aren't sailing the sea of life alone." He waited a moment before slowly bringing his legs to a ninety-degree angle, pausing, then uncurling, in perfect control of his body. "Are we running a caper today, Beppo, or are we going to waste the day?"

Elizabeth wished she could still drink it all in the way Beppo did.

His face flushed with excitement, Beppo cleared his throat. "No more diversionary tactics, we're here to concentrate on the caper at hand. Hypothesis: Can we spend the entire day without coughing up a cent, while going downtown, having lunch, going to a movie —"

"Refined people say film, Beppo." Elizabeth shook her hair down her back, but it never worked for her the way it did for Wendy. The end of Elizabeth's thick braid swatted her cheek.

Beppo grinned mindlessly. Two months and he was still an outsider. "OK, March sixth, official caper has begun, you will have three full hours to complete the caper, do not depend on your neighbor for the correct answers, turn in your assorted valuables." They tossed him money, change, Crunch's signet ring.

Beppo arranged their money with the absorption of a painter assembling a still life. Of course the group was rating his performance. "Today's rules are simple — the scam is to take the bus down, lunch at Sampson's, then a *flick*." He toppled the coins in Elizabeth's direction.

Beppo wished one of them would step outside the caper long enough to explain the point of the whole thing. They couldn't be getting a high from sneaking into the movies like cheap punks. Beppo so wanted to be perfect, undetectable from the real ones. But he still quaked in Tess Goldman's immaculate living room. He would be struck dumb when she asked him in her purring voice if his mother made her linguini from scratch. Reviewing his progress each evening on the ferry, he was dogged by the fact that he had years left at home, years when jokes about Aunt Rosalie baking cakes for her weekly Weight Watchers meetings were considered wit.

"We are five as one," Peter sang out as they walked in step across 86th Street.

Crunch automatically responded whenever Peter spoke. "Subway home, mates? Got them big-deal guards now. More of a challenge than the pokey old bus."

Beppo sometimes despaired of ever catching up with them. But he applied the same intense concentration to memorizing their moves as he did to applied set theory. And prayed to St. Anthony for success.

At no time did Wendy feel the breathless excitement a caper provided, even an old one like capering a whole day without money. Only Wendy performed solo capers, for the feeling of power it gave her to pit herself all alone against the entire city. "What about we hit Bloomie's, quintessential emporium of banality. Women stagger out of there as though they've seen a vision of the blessed St. Lucy." She genuflected in Beppo's direction and crossed herself.

Walking between Peter and Crunch, Elizabeth willed Kate to the back of her mind. The magic overtook her. She was clever as Crunch, moody as Peter. She moved with Wendy's grace. She reached over and smacked Beppo's leg. "You're a quick study, Ace, doin' a good job."

"OK, get it together," Beppo said, his voice gaining in authority. "Don't want the driver to get his hackles up. We aren't surly teenagers, we're good citizens, good *Americans*."

When the bus nosed into the curb at Times Square,

Crunch socked Peter's hip. Wendy crowed as she jumped down from the bus and fell against Beppo. It had been too long since their last caper.

"Moving right along." Crunch lifted Elizabeth under her armpits and danced her a few steps.

Wendy whispered in disgust to Beppo, "Crunch may explode in the restaurant. You're in charge, act in charge."

"You think one large table might call attention to us?" Beppo asked uneasily.

"If it were safe, Vincent, we wouldn't be doing it," Elizabeth said with exaggerated patience.

Wendy hugged Elizabeth. "Cheer up. The funeral is over. Good times ahead. We're all together just like —" Wendy waited for one of the others to finish her statement. Crunch and Peter shrugged.

"Mickey and Minnie Mouse. Christ, I'm talking like Kate Callahan and she's still in Boston," Elizabeth pushed through the door to Sampson's. "Do you have a table large enough for all of us?" she purred to the hostess.

Wendy ran her hands through her hair and followed close behind the hostess. "We took the bus in from Jersey to catch a movie." The hostess counted out five menus, smiled perfunctorily and left.

"You asshole. If anything goes wrong, she'll remember the blond kid in the tan suede jacket. *The bus in from Jersey.* Can't you stand being anonymous, even to a goddam waitress?"

"Don't use that tone with me, Peter Zeiss," Wendy said, filled with righteousness, her face tight as a knot.

"How come Vigilante Tippett lets Wendybird go to school with common folk?" Beppo had waited so long to ask that question. From what he had pieced together from scraps of conversation, Wendy's father had the suspicions of a redneck, but Vinnie had never heard of a millionaire redneck.

"Daddy Cash didn't know there were such kinds at Demaret. By the time he found out, Wendy'd already been exposed, contaminated —" Elizabeth explained in her expressionless tone.

"Oh he's sly, my daddy, always a step ahead of the pack. If he sends me to school with Jews, he doesn't have to worry about black folks, cause Jews ain't about to cut anybody into their action."

Vinnie looked furtively at Peter, but the line about Jews didn't even cause him to blink. Anybody mouthed a slur about Italians around Pop, the old boy would sock 'em in the jaw. Beppo suspected if he came out with a crack like Wendy's, Peter would definitely react.

"Not to put too fine a point on it," Crunch said, wearing his bored look, "but Demaret is hardly common folk. Until you graced our portals, Beppo my boy, we had nobody more exotic than Lenore's Hindu guru to feed Tippett's paranoia."

"Well, moving right along." Beppo's voice sounded strained in his own ears. "Here's how we execute the caper. As soon as we finish eating, Elizabeth, you go to the john and wait there for five minutes. Peter waits by the jukebox to slip into the men's —"

"Enough, Beppo, today is practice for *you*. We have been capering since long before you were born." Crunch's heart wasn't in it. Today's caper was merely killing time until Kate Callahan arrived. He had to exercise restraint.

If he weren't exceptionally cool, the group would realize he really dug her, and they'd insist he give her up.

It was fine for him to escort her to the Faculty Dance at Columbia last year, after all Peter took Elizabeth, and he was doing Lizzie a favor by squiring her lamentable cousin. He'd been totally unprepared for Kate Callahan. He'd thought she'd be a disagreeable version of Elizabeth. Instead, she was the best-looking girl in the ballroom, and she could dance to any kind of music. Crunch had suppressed his own desire to dance because it was considered by the group to be one of those conventional dead ends they avoided. But that night he danced for hours, and got credit for being a sport in the bargain.

Fortunately the Goldmans were sending Kate to Beaver, across town from Demaret. So the group would not be able to observe him with Kate. He was in the pole position as it stood now. Meeting her plane tonight established that. If Elizabeth got suspicious about his attentions to Kate, he'd throw it right back at her, pointing out her two-bit jealousy until everybody pressured Elizabeth to penance herself. And what would be a more fitting punishment than demanding that Crunch spend as much time as possible at Kate's side?

There was no way he could lose. Not that he had any dark plans for the girl. Kate was hardly the sort to screw in a dingy humid room on Upper Broadway. He'd had one of those last summer. He'd picked her up in Riverside Park one afternoon while everybody was out of town. He and the girl had walked uptown along the river. She had a large shoulder bag that rattled when she walked. When they all came home from vacations, he had not mentioned the girl. If he had described her cheap sling-back shoes, her sooty eye makeup, they'd have recoiled. If he had told them about the apartment over Bertha's Bakery where he'd spent those afternoons, they'd have censored him for foraging in the park. Even if he had made it clear that it was a purely physical thing, he had never bought her dinner or taken her to a museum, he suspected they'd resent his thrusting his hand into the cookie jar the minute they were out of town. He felt damn lucky to get out of it without her learning his real name.

Crunch studied Beppo's face as he ate his cheeseburger. His eyes were shining with eagerness. He'd probably been in and out of the cookie jar so often he could be considered a sexual diabetic.

Beppo thought he was getting the hang of it. He sounded more like Crunch these days than Peter did. "Wendy will insist to the box-office broad that she *absolutely* gave her a ten, where is her ticket and where is her change? Then Wendy passes me the box-office bread with which I shall buy a legitimate ticket."

"Note who gets in safe and sound," Elizabeth spoke to the bowl of pickles.

Beppo could imagine no encounter grisly enough to make him quit the group. Even the bloody combination of his old man and his brother Louis throwing him around like a bocci ball if he was ever caught seemed an acceptable risk. Eternal Vigilance had lost its allure. Being one of them was its own absolution.

Elizabeth, too restless to sit through lunch, walked to the front of the restaurant. Let someone else spend Beppo's well-timed minutes in the can. She paused in front of wicker baskets filled with fruit and candy, encased in orange cellophane. Just the thing for Crunch to carry to the airport.

She waited until several people had lined up in front of the cashier's cage. She picked up a basket, then decided on the one behind it. The grapes were bigger. She cast a quick look at the exits and threw her shoulder against the revolving door. She knew the group was breathless.

The cool air revived her. She set the basket beside her and leaned against the window of the shoe store to wait. The rest of the day was hers.

Wendy cheered. Crunch danced down the street with the basket.

"Score! Score!" Peter held up Elizabeth's arm.

"That sure was the hat trick," Beppo said admiringly.

Elizabeth was surprised to find the apartment dark. To think she hustled them all back uptown immediately after the movie. She had been certain Tess would be home whipping up some delicacy for KC's first night in New York. Since they'd returned from the funeral, Tess had been as inviting as a lunar landscape.

"You know, Tessa," Sam had said after frowning at the ceiling for a long time, "if the speed of the car had changed plus or minus three miles an hour —"

Tess pulled the drapes closed, cutting off the view of the Hudson, violet in the dense March dusk. She turned on several lamps.

"Or if the other car had left point y instead of point

x —" He was inscribing jottings on the air, his finger moving like a pencil.

"Don't reduce my sister's death to a formula, Sam."

"Sam only meant —"

"I know what he meant. I don't need any help from you. And while we're on the subject, I expect you to be very careful around Kate."

"God forbid she might have to mourn right through dinner." Elizabeth held her breath and squinted at her mother.

But Tess picked up a magazine and sat down, composed and aloof as if she were in a waiting room among strangers.

Elizabeth stalked down the hall, filled with rage at the memory of her mother's frozen control. Her anger frothed up suddenly like chemicals in a test tube. Tess was probably out buying presents for Kate. She rubbed her face against the rough wool of her sweater. They can shop together 'til they've worn their legs to stumps, Elizabeth thought. At least Kate won't fool Wendy and the boys with her breathy purity. Grinning, Elizabeth put Mahler's Second Symphony on the stereo in Sam's study and turned the volume up until the chords resounded throughout the apartment. She sat on the couch in the living room, rubbing the soles of her sneakers against Tess's ivory upholstery.

When Tess was home, Elizabeth listened to music with earphones in her room, so her mother couldn't patronize her right back to kindergarten. Tess made listening to a symphony or sonata an occasion for developing Elizabeth's ear: Now what is the phrasing? Can you hear the oboe?

Sam spoke in the elusive language of equations and measurements. When they took Sunday walks to the Boat Basin through the park, Sam would spin countless problems. If a train is leaving Chicago at 7:30 and travels east at 90 miles an hour, if I had a gross of bath towels and you had three bathtubs, if a monkey and a half spent a dollar and a half. Even under the open sky of the park, Elizabeth felt crushed by their knowledge. From the time she learned to read, she sensed that the way to shore up her end was books. The test wasn't if she could solve Sam's riddles or identify a Bach cantata, but how fast she could come up with the answer.

Tonight high on the success of the day's caper, Elizabeth did not begrudge her mother her victories over the financial board; the visiting conductor from Milan; her closet where no dress hung spotted, missing a button, half-hemmed. Tonight she would start dinner as a gesture of sympathy toward Tess. Her mother's feelings usually eluded Elizabeth. She seemed so angry at Aunt Janet for dying. But Elizabeth had noticed that since the night of the phone call Tess's face had developed fine lines, like cobwebs, of sadness.

Having Kate around twenty-four hours a day would be no day at the beach. A day at the beach! Elizabeth thought back to the summers on Cape Ann, when Kate, smooth-skinned and tan, would run down the beach in pursuit of a sandpiper, or run into the waves without checking to make sure an adult was watching, without checking the ferocity of the undertow. No, Kate had never had the panoply of fears that had ruled Elizabeth's childhood — even on vacation.

Elizabeth sat on the kitchen stool and studied Tess's menu: "Sat. Eve.: veal, spaghetti carbonara, salad, spinach soufflé." She took the package labeled veal from the meat compartment, washed the spinach leaves, and put a pot of salted water on to boil for the spaghetti. She wondered if Mrs. Santini could cook Italian as well as Tessa.

Crunch would continue to tease her about Kate. In spite of his loyalty to her, Elizabeth knew Crunch couldn't resist a terrific looking girl. She'd followed his gaze when a knockout model type walked by; she'd noticed how he contrived to walk next to Wendy when the four of them were going anywhere. She could hardly blame him.

Kate learned things so easily. Diving under waves, and never getting caught in the curl, instinctively wrapping a beach towel sarong-style around her athletic body while Elizabeth huddled under the beach umbrella, swathed in towels, squinting at the lovely picture her cousin made. At least she doesn't live near me in the winter, the twelve-year-old Elizabeth consoled herself.

And now Kate was going to cast her shadow over everyone Elizabeth cared about. Even this afternoon Crunch had been unable to disguise his real pleasure at Kate's arrival. And Wendy had picked up on it. "Remember when you refused to eat the school lunch in first grade, Crunch?" Wendy's gentle tone hardened. It's still a surprise, Elizabeth thought, Wendy's Olivia Newton-John face coupled with her wicked ability to cut through us with the power of a chainsaw.

Crunch's face grew cautious. Wendy continued. "You cried because the meat was touching the potatoes and your peas were floating in the gravy? You're not going to

45

try to mix everyone up in one stew — honey-luscious KC and us?"

"She couldn't pass the physical, Tippett. You know, the part where we all dance on the head of a pin?" Crunch thrust his hands out to Wendy, making the fingers of his right hand dance on the palm of his left. Crunch always recovered quickly, no matter how slippery the ground.

Elizabeth looked at the clock. Her momentary urge to action — to begin dinner and take the lead in the Sunflower-Kate celebration — had fizzled. Since when did a sane individual welcome her replacement?

But the nagging aura of death would not go away. It was hard to keep in mind that her aunt and uncle were really dead. When Grandfather had died, he'd been sick for a long time and everyone was prepared. When her other grandparents had died, she'd been very young. Tess and Sam didn't talk about them much. When they did, it seemed no different from when they discussed characters from a favorite book.

Aunt Janet had had the same glow that Kate had. Aunt Janet was only twenty years older than Elizabeth. I could be dead in twenty years, or ten years, or five, she thought. Wendy and the boys would go to college, get jobs, win the Nobel Prize, without Elizabeth being there. Even in a dream, even if she was pretending to be dead, it was more like she was hidden from view. She could watch them living without them knowing she was there. But not to be there at all — it was too awful to imagine.

The front door opened. Hearing Tess's Hello, Elizabeth lunged toward her bedroom and closed the door. She fingered the gray flannel of her three-year-old jumper,

46

and turned away from the mirror. She dressed like a British matron in an Alec Guinness movie. Good-sense Elizabeth with a closet full of cotton turtlenecks and jeans. About as sexy as a vacuum cleaner. She's not even here yet and she's making me dissatisfied with every square inch of my life. Elizabeth grabbed a handful of hangers. Cursing under her breath, she marched down the hall to her parents' room.

"Give these hangers to KC. She'll be disoriented if she has three more pretty shirts than hangers."

Tess sighed and opened her closet door. She took a blue wool dress off its hanger and slipped it over her head. "There's so much to do. Poor Kate, she must feel so alone. I want you to make a special effort —" Tess closed the closet door. "We'll need to build bookshelves in the kitchen for all Sam's books. With Kate living in the spare room, and his study already overflowing, the poor man will have no place to spread out." She shook her head as though shaking water out of her ear. "Can't be helped."

"You'll be gaining a wardrobe, which should be some compensation for losing the spare room," Elizabeth said. Why couldn't she come right out and say "May I borrow one of your dresses, so I could look nice tonight?" Whenever she talked to her mother, even the simplest compliments or requests turned sour in her mouth.

"Plane's due at six. She and Crunch should get here by seven, and we'll eat right away. Sam's exhausted. Kate will need to unpack and settle in. I've got a briefcase full of work."

"Crunch may have other plans."

"Why are you so gloomy? You've been out larking all

day. You didn't even ask if I could use your help this morning before you shot out of here." Tess glanced at herself in the mirror and smoothed her hair with the flat of her hand.

"Usually you tell me you'd rather do it yourself, unless it's taking out the trash or doing the laundry. You know, the fun stuff."

"You can make a salad. The lettuce is washed, the radishes and scallions are not. Put the half red pepper in too. Will Crunch be expecting dinner?"

"I'm not an expert on what Crunch expects."

"I have only two pounds of veal. I'll fill in with extra spaghetti. OK, I'll make the salad. You run to Ruggio's and get some fresh *parmegiano*."

"What difference does it make? Crunch doesn't eat much."

"Once, I'd like a conversation with you that does not become a debate. Veal's six dollars a pound. Is it unreasonable if I want to know how many people to *buy* for? I am not running a restaurant."

"You're not unreasonable, Tess. I am. Crunch will probably be delighted to feast on golden veal and golden Kate."

"It's five-thirty," Tess said. She stifled the desire to hit her daughter by throwing a pencil across the room. "Forget Ruggio's."

"I'll go, Tess. Right away."

Elizabeth went to her room for her canvas bag. She lugged it everywhere. Aside from the money, keys, lip gloss (she carried it faithfully but never used it), notebooks, several felt-tip pens, there were always one or two books she chose for every journey, even a five-minute errand.

Tess was waiting at the front door, her look indicating she was being kept from important duties. "Here's some cash. Better wear a scarf. Pick up an extra pound of butter."

"I'm warm enough and I have money."

The elevator door opened. Tess held the door open with her foot. "You must have an immense amount of reading to do. You're averaging twenty bucks a month at the bookstore. You don't read half those books, do you?"

Elizabeth held herself immobile until the door slid closed. Then she socked the wall with her lumpy bookbag. "Bitch! Mistress of Dismissals. Her unending lists! Five-thirty chop up Elizabeth. Six-thirty welcome Kate. Six-thirty-three inform Crunch Maxwell veal is six dollars a pound." Elizabeth wrapped both arms around her canvas bag and strode through the lobby, ignoring Hector the doorman's cheery hello as he opened the door for her.

As she turned the corner toward Ruggio's she glanced in at Marty's Meats. When she was little, she used to write her name in sawdust on Marty's floor. She could sit on the little marble ledge across from Marty watching him hack up chickens and slabs of beef for hours. But Tess didn't shop there and fretted that Elizabeth was a nuisance to the butcher.

From Marty's, Elizabeth moved her base of operations to the bookstores in the neighborhood. Because they lived near Columbia University, there were plenty of bookstores. She liked to walk down the cobblestone paths near her father's lab, carrying a book cover side out. Sometimes selecting a book, putting it on her night table, carrying it around with her, weaving the title or author into a conversation with Wendy and the boys was as gratifying as reading the book. She assumed girls who were attracted to cosmetic counters felt the same way about tempting shades of lipstick.

Tess's voice eddied around her daughter, closing out the impatient blasts of rush-hour car horns. Elizabeth opened the door to the vegetable market and waved at the man behind the counter.

"A hunk of Parmesan and a pound of butter."

"For Mrs. Goldman, *bellissima!* And she goin' to grate it herself. She always tell me, Mario, there is no man in this town can pick melon like you. What a nice lady, you mother!"

"I'm kind of in a hurry."

"Look what just come in. Arugula, fresh from the ground this morning. Still damp."

"She's already made a salad."

"She always want arugula. What else she making?"

"I'm not sure."

"Look at these oranges, Indian River. Very tough to get because of that freeze they having in Florida."

"Just cheese and butter. That's all she wants."

"Tell your mother to wrap wet paper towel around arugula and it will keep fresh one week."

"How much is all that?"

He waved his hands impatiently. "When she come in, your mama pay."

Car headlights shone mean out of the darkness. Elizabeth touched her hair, smoothed it behind her ears. Three black kids walked alongside her, shrieking with laughter. Elizabeth reversed direction and decided to take the long way home. She clutched her bag more tightly. Her lips compressed, she looked away from the traffic. She couldn't bear Crunch, Peter, and even Beppo tossing her aside like a pencil stub for a chance at Kate, that feeble-minded crowd pleaser. Welcome to my life, it's all yours, KC.

Elizabeth tossed her braid over her shoulder and walked faster. She kicked a crumpled milk carton into the gutter. A wave of onion and garlic floated in the air outside the pizza stand. Elizabeth closed her eyes against the blistering vision of KC running toward her in the sensual rhythm of a mouthwash commercial, wisps of cinnamon-colored hair blowing across her American-beauty face. Face it, she's going to walk into Tess and Sam's comforting arms, not to mention Crunch's expectant ones, and old wooden Lizard will be as sought after as a bathtub ring.

Elizabeth ran through the lobby, loathing herself for her melodramatic thoughts. Why couldn't she feel the sadness it was normal to feel when members of your family die suddenly? She vowed to be compassionate with Kate, but even as she thought it, she felt a knot of stubbornness deep within.

"What's happenin', Elizabeth?" Hector flashed his ever-ready smile.

"My cousin's coming to live here."

"Thas nice."

"Her parents were killed last week."

"The Lord give and the Lord take away."

"Right. You want to taste something delicious?" She reached into her bag. "Nibble this with your dinner, or bring it home to your wife."

"Thank you. What you call it?"

"Arugula. Fresh today. Very special."

"*This is Bunny Oliver outside Washington High School in New York City. We've got our mobile unit here, just a few blocks from the subway station where one teenage girl met her death last night. Behind me are some students from Washington High School. Let's hear what they think happened last night.*"

"*They didn't give out the girl's name. Could be someone went to school with us. I called all my girl-friends after I heard the news to be sure it wasn't one of them.*"

"*Me too!*"

"*I did too!*"

"*I knew it wasn't one of my friends. 'Cause we never get near that platform, all those freaks out there, specially on the Broadway train. I take the A train whenever I can.*"

"*They got freaks on the A train too. You see those kids ridin' on the last car, and they be leanin' over, holdin' on with one hand. Some of them ride all the way to Brooklyn like that. Surprised one of them don't get crushed.*"

"*I heard of one did. And then remember the kid who was pulled onto the track by someone hanging out the window of the train? Reached right out and snatched her arm.*"

"*They said on the news some boys was with the girl. Probably was her boyfriend got jealous or something.*"

"*Some boyfriend!*"

4

Crunch wanted Kate Callahan the way he had once wanted a horse. He rolled over and buried his face in his pillow, rocking from side to side. Kate living three blocks north on Riverside Drive!

Things had gotten tense at the airport. She had looked grand in a purple dress printed with tiny pink flowers. While they were waiting for the crowd to thin out at the taxi stand, he had bought her some coffee.

"We're all so glad you're here. I mean, sure is a lousy break and all for you, but for us it's good."

At first she smiled, flattered by his attention. She didn't pull away when he held her hand. Then out of the blue, her eyes got swimmy.

"Sorry, Crunch, it's only been a week. You know, my mind hasn't caught up with my feelings."

She was into full-fledged tears. In the middle of a coffee shop. People were eyeing him as though he were the cause of her sadness. He'd never known a kid with no parents. Kids with one parent were becoming as common at Demaret as Space Invaders freaks. Of course there was

54

Peter, who was parented long distance. Crunch hadn't a clue about the right thing to say to Kate.

"Dinner is ready, Simon." Mrs. Maxwell stood in the doorway of his room. He caught her frowning at his down jacket on the floor. He sprang off his bed causing her to back up a few steps. The most important element in Crunch's contest with his mother was speed. With exquisite skill and flash, he won round after round.

"We're having spaghetti," she said dully.

"How Italianissimo!" He grinned and patted her on the back as though she'd just won a round of *Family Feud*.

Dinner gave Crunch a daily opportunity to exercise his swordsmanship.

"You look kind of wispy, Daddy."

"He's our robust Pa, Gina my gumdrop. The men in this family are all robust and pretty near perfect." Crunch didn't look up from the spaghetti hanging in loops half-down his chin.

From the time she could say his name (Gina was the only one who'd call him Crunch, his parents refused to), Gina was his. Even now, when she was so involved with her dancing classes, she lived to please him. Family dinners were high times. He and Gina had always been a joint act. Last night she'd been talking about her school's spring dance recital.

"If the star were to meet with an accident, would they let the star's multitalented brother go on in her tutu?"

"Don't tease your sister, Simon," Mrs. Maxwell said from behind her silver fish platter.

"It's OK, Mom, I'd rather have him tease me than act

cross with me." Gina raised her milk glass and toasted him. "I'd rather hear Crunch than overhear him."

"Whatever does that mean?" Mrs. Maxwell asked, a spot of alarm in her eyes.

"You just remember who loves you, Gina," Crunch said, leaning way back in his chair.

Jerry Maxwell pushed back his chair and clasped his hands in a jovial manner. "Spaghetti was delicious, my dear. Simon, would you come into my study? I want to talk to you about something."

Crunch loathed the study. Its walls were covered with pale imitation suede, like a gigantic calf's nostril. Darker suede covered a couch and several chairs. They were such Babbitts, his father buying a new car every two years. The Goldmans had abandoned their old Peugeot because they didn't want to waste another dollar shoring it up. Professor Goldman spoke wryly about a technology that could grind a telescopic lense $\pm$ .005 of accuracy and refused to construct a sturdy automobile. Crunch's father accepted that his car door rattled and engine knocked. As long as the stereo worked and the upholstery was soft, he was satisfied.

Crunch thought his mother would embrace whatever gadget the stores were pushing. She was why Ralph Nader was in business, although she wouldn't be warned away from something she really wanted. He watched her eyes as she flipped through the Sunday paper, checking the ads framed by columns of dull gray news. But all in all, Crunch was grateful for cash flow. Long as it flowed, Mrs. Maxwell would remain too preoccupied to gum up his life.

"Simon dear, would you like a piece of fruit?" his mother asked. One thing about her that he approved was her soft, slightly hesitant voice. She phrased everything as a question. "There're some very nice apples?"

"Better go check out what Dad wants." He turned at the door and crossed swiftly to his mother's chair. He kissed her lightly on the top of her head.

"OK, Dad, what's the problem?" Private chats were not his father's style. Whatever he had to say could be said between TV shows. "Bet Mom insists that God carpet Heaven celery green to match her upholstery, which you know she is sending by UPS."

"She'll phone ahead to make sure," Jerry Maxwell agreed. His father's nervous laugh meant he was ill at ease. This will take five minutes tops, Crunch thought as his father stood up and walked over to his desk, anxiously looking for some papers.

"What I have to say is very difficult. A father never wants to lose rating points in his son's estimation."

"What the hell does that mean?" Crunch grew wary; this didn't sound like his father.

"A man does his best for his family, exercises good judgment, wants to give everything to his loved ones, that is, after all, what life is all about —"

"Could we skip the crapola?"

"The end-of-the-year accounting is in. The picture is bleak."

"What are you talking about? One, two, three."

"We're going to be tight for money, some investments —"

"How tight?"

"We're tapped out, only as far as cash flow, you understand."

"You mean Maxwell Ink, your hotshot ad agency, has dried up?"

"Of course not. But our expenses were astronomical this year with the new graphics computer, and we've all had to plow earnings back into the company. And the accountants tell me we're going to be strapped, megastrapped." He looked at the clock. They had been talking four minutes. "So when we got this letter from Headmaster Withers about college applications, I thought now is as good a time as any to tell you to fill out some forms for a scholarship."

Crunch's hard gaze followed his father's hands gliding over the tooled leather surface of the desk nobody used. "What about the apartment and the Rockland house?"

"Nothing has to change. It's cash flow, I told you."

"Screw cash flow."

"Watch your mouth, young man."

"Watch your wallet! You tell me to forget college and I should watch my mouth. Oh Boy!"

"You'll win a scholarship. You'd be an asset to any school. I am not a bit worried. I wanted to tell you now so you could maximize your opportunities. Explore every avenue . . ."

"You're not worried? An asset? They don't give money to WASP boys anymore. They want girls, blacks, first-generation like Beppo. His old man *works* for a living." Crunch heard his jaw snap. "Why don't you sell the damn Rockland house? We only use it weekends."

"Your mother would be lost without her garden. Don't look so hopeless, old boy. All kids come a little unglued when it comes time to apply to college."

"Don't you realize there is a real world, where they don't give money to kids like me because their fathers have a hole in their wallets? You shouldn't have kids if you can't pay for them, isn't that what they tell folks on welfare?"

"OK, slugger, we'll talk about it another time."

"Forget the whole business. I'll deal with it myself. But don't ever give me the old hustle, about my education and Gina's being the first order of business." He broke off, aware that he had the advantage. He stormed out of the room, never looking back at his father.

Thursday night had become Wendy's favorite night of the week. It was her caper night. Last time she'd made the *Times*. Tonight she was hoping for some mention on *Good Morning America*. To sit at breakfast knowing David Hartman was actually talking about her. What an extraordinary caper. Beppo had looked so solemn when he left her this afternoon. "Don't worry, Beppo, I'll be close to God!" She'd laughed at his wide-eyed gasp. The others were more than a little impressed with her daring. Gradually she was taking the lead. She paused to look in a store window. She heard somebody's radio blaring; she saw several people running to catch the bus. Then the street noises retreated and the people became stick figures, like those on Beppo's beloved video games, jerking their way across the street. Everything was going her way.

59

The moment passed. Wendy's hand closed over the can of spray paint in her jacket pocket. She tied a scarf over her head and yanked open the door of St. Jean of the Holy Martyr. She dipped her fingers into the baptismal font and spread a few drops of water across her lips. There were about a dozen women kneeling in the pews nearest the altar. She walked down the aisle and genuflected, bowing her head 'til it almost touched the floor. She turned and walked to the rear of the church, her eyes fixed on the vacant choir loft.

As she left the church, she pulled the can from her pocket, gave one quick glance over her shoulder, and scrawled on the heavy wooden doors: God is dead.

Peter suspected Lenore and Benny weren't coming back. But unlike Kate he couldn't expect any sympathy. He had grown to hate the empty apartment. If he painted the living room bright purple Lenore'd say wonderful my darling, bet you feel like a grape. He could drop dead at her feet and she would dash outside and scan the sky, hoping to see his soul traveling toward another reality.

He checked his watch. Seven minutes after seven. He slipped the latch on the door. Gina would arrive in twenty minutes. She'd probably wear her seagull T-shirt. He rang the elevator button. With any luck Gina would be there when he got back with the wine. He heard the phone ring, but did not go back to answer it. At this hour it would be Lenore. Even if he did die, her strident voice would reach him. There she would be at her own kid's funeral, probably wearing jeans and some weird beaded top. Lenore was incapable of dressing like a mother. She'd certainly wear her favorite ring — the one she'd made during her jewelry period — it was made from his and Andy's baby teeth.

His funeral would be another chance for her to brag about her sons, the best, my boys, what a reflection on me! Her hands scampering all over the place, she'd push that idiot Tippett a few heartbeats closer to a massive coronary. "There's nothing my boys hold back from me. Media's full of crap, this business about generation gap! I have a close relationship with both my boys. They trust me because I never hold anything back. I give it to them straight, no kiddy version of life." Just like Lenore to forget he'd died.

With Benny she always came out swinging. She'd drop her voice to its huskiest tones, but still loud enough for Benny to hear every syllable. "You boys must not repress what your father is, or you'll become *macho* too. Let us empty our minds of this world," she'd say and slide down to the floor, tugging on their wrists to sit down too. She would arrange herself in the lotus. And with Benny pretending to read the paper, she'd smile dreamily at her sons. "Now, darlings, sit here. That's right; no, close your eyes, breathe in, *hold it,* breathe out. Now we can meditate."

Peter ran down the two flights of stairs to save time. If the Maxwells ate early tonight Gina would be on her way. He had started teaching her yoga. He could tell her how much he enjoyed waking up at dawn to do his yoga and meditation routine every morning. But he could not tell Wendy, who scoffed at such things. He could not defend yoga without defending his mother.

Wendy had been home about twenty minutes when the doorbell rang. She ran to answer it before her father heard it and lectured whoever was standing in the hall about dropping in unannounced. Usually after dinner Wendy's parents retreated to their bedroom, which had a tiny refrigerator and bar, a TV and stereo system separate from the one in the living room, two bathrooms and two dressing rooms. Lily often said they could stay in there for days if the need arose without missing any of the amenities.

Elizabeth, looking like a gorgon with her hair unbraided, was pacing the hall in front of the Tippett's door.

"Who's chasing you?" Wendy, flushed with the victory of her caper, stepped out of Elizabeth's path. She was carrying her canvas bookbag over her shoulder, slightly stooped, like one of the dwarfs coming home to Snow White.

"Been at the library. Closes at nine on Thursdays now. Finished taking notes for my history paper. It's too hard working at home with God's gift to the Goldmans fumbling through math. Tess insists I help her." Elizabeth picked at Wendy's candlewick bedspread, puckering the fabric, then pressing it flat. "Who would've figured Kate Callahan would become the white man's burden?"

Wendy itched to soak Elizabeth's broad knuckles in

oil, shape her nails, put some shine on her. Might as well ask her to work as a stripper. She was unadorned and so virtuous about it.

"You're ten times the girl Kate is. Can't you believe we all love you, the boys and me? Like always."

"It isn't *me* Beppo loves."

"You're the most vain girl I know."

"Me, the Prunella Plain of Demaret?"

"You're vain about me, it's part of your poor-old-Elizabeth number."

Elizabeth sighed. "You're right. I imagine all these guys are in love with you." And trying to go to bed with you at every possible opportunity, she thought. You'll never know what it feels like to be overlooked.

"Don't forget we've all forsworn our classmates, our relatives, our neighbors — doesn't leave too many folks," Wendy said.

"You'll never suggest to the boys that KC should join, like we took Beppo?"

"Could we cork KC? She's not the tidal wave you're predicting!" Wendy was exasperated. Why couldn't Elizabeth see that Kate was a well-balanced breakfast, and boys are never lured to what is good for them.

"I'm sorry," whispered Elizabeth. She feared that cold look in Wendy's eyes.

"Anyway, we sure don't need members. We all live in each other's pockets."

"She'll find plenty of admirers at Beaver," Elizabeth said. "Tess deserves the Humanitarian of the Year award for sending her to Beaver." Elizabeth saw by Wendy's irritated sighs that she'd better change direction. "It'll be fun to watch Crunch come on to her. Think he'll play it suave like Redford or clumsy like Woody Allen?"

"You're right about one thing. When it comes to Kate, he'll be playing. Crunch doesn't care two licks about her. Don't you know he's *us*, more than anyone! He'll never get involved with an outsider."

"One of us is bound to get involved sooner or later." Elizabeth felt odd saying aloud what she had feared so often.

"We will always be us if we want to be. It's what we've always worked toward. We'll never fall for that dating razzle. I love the boys, I love you, I love us."

Elizabeth had such difficulty with the word *love*. "I suppose you're right. But each year it takes more vigilance to keep us together — just us five, five as one."

"When you say it that way, I see you in robes, splashing us with Holy water," Wendy told her. "Maybe you'll be an abbess and purify all of us."

"How did it go tonight?"

"Without a hitch. I even went into the sanctuary first. And I didn't wait until the coast was clear."

"The sanctuary! You are cutting it closer!"

"After the next couple of Thursdays I'll quit. Each week it gets easier. You perform any caper enough times, it loses its excitement."

"But you've done this one five times already!"

"How dare you question me about a caper!" Wendy bit off each word.

Elizabeth swung her bookbag over her shoulder. She

was having to defuse Wendy more and more frequently.

"Don't be ridiculous, Wendy pet. I know better than that. You have more guts than the rest of us put together. Especially Beppo. Bet he's been bargaining all night with Uncle God. Beppo will give away his place on the heavenly bread line for one taste —" she raised her eyebrows and rang for the elevator — "of your *soul!*"

Wendy lunged at Elizabeth, who sidestepped her and leaned against the wall, a slight smile on her face. Wendy's fury grew. "I've had it with your mind always on my body," Wendy hissed. "You're lucky it's Peter's week to prescribe penance. Lately he's been sloppy. Next time it's my week. I may very well insist you get it on with one of Beppo's sweaty relatives."

Elizabeth clenched her trembling hands. "I was only kidding."

"Don't look so stricken. I was kidding too. But you'd better tell Peter you got on me about the cathedral. By the way, you can tell him tonight was St. Jean of the Holy Martyr." She put her arms around Elizabeth's waist. "I love you, sorry I lost my temper. Just the fallout after a caper."

"Hello, you." Peter rested his hand in Gina's hair. He kissed her first because she loved him, would wait around for an hour if he was out with his friends, then he kissed her for saying he was the gift of her life, he was her everything, then he clutched her hair, squeezed it in his fists because he wanted to feel every minute with her, because he knew he was beginning to tire of her all-the-time sweetness.

65

"Hey, you're hurting me."

"Not if you think of it as love," he told her and pushed her back roughly onto the bed.

She put her arms around him and held him tight. He had told her that a boy feels physical pain unless he is satisfied. She held him all the time his body shook in such incomprehensible spasms.

"That was the best," Peter said a while later. He was tracing the pattern of Gina's ear with his fingertip when the phone rang. He stretched toward the receiver, silently cursing whoever was tearing him from this time. Gina smiled sleepily. "I've got to get home. It's so late — they'll have fits. Crunch had some big pow-wow with Dad. I left before it was over. You know Crunch, he'll say I deserted him." She licked his fingers. "Coming to Rockland with us this weekend?"

The phone rang again.

"Don't go yet, I'll get rid of whoever it is in a second. Hello, you've got the wrong number."

Frantically motioning Gina to rejoin him on the bed, he nodded several times and grunted into the phone. "What do you plan to do about it?"

Gina blew him a kiss from the door.

"No, damn it, Elizabeth, I'm not in the midde of anything." The door slammed. "What would I be doing for God's sake? How could you twit Wendy about a caper? Suppose Curtis had overheard? You know how he sneaks around that place, wouldn't be surprised if he's got Wendy's room bugged."

"I thought I'd have a little get-together, all of us, and some of the kids from Beaver, as a way to cheer up Kate.

I must start being kinder to her. Wendy pointed out to me that I've been acting very jealous lately, and I know she's right."

"Excellent, Elizabeth," Peter said, genuinely pleased.

"Prices rose sharply on the big board yesterday, trading was mixed. In the race for the Stanley Cup, the Rangers moved a step closer, trouncing the Bruins six to two. This item just in. The vandals who defaced the doors of St. Patrick's Cathedral last week struck again last night. Father James Wheeler of St. Jean of the Holy Martyr spoke to our Hugo Lawton just a few moments ago. 'We would have thought this a silly prank except that God is dead *was scrawled in the same swirly script as the doors last week and the three previous weeks. Green spray paint was used, and so far, we have no clue to the identity of the criminal, or his intentions. The police are beefing up their force, so we can only pray the deranged mind who has been doing this will be caught very, very soon.' "*

"What kind of nut is loose? Another Fascist Communist that's who. Defacing the church. Vincent, eat that egg." His mother slid a fried egg onto his plate. "It loses its good if it gets cold."

Vinnie's ears were burning. He gripped his knife and fork tightly to disguise his quivering hands.

"They need tougher laws for these kids. Lock them in jail, have whippings in public, like they do in Italy, then they won't scoff at the law, a few beatings make sure the children grow up proper, right, Vinnie?"

"You'd better believe it, Pop." Why was the old man so

67

sure it was a kid, why couldn't it be someone like him, a house painter making a statement?

"It's a good thing we have Vinnie in that school. With nice kids."

He wished he could tell them his friends called him Beppo.

Run a block, walk a block was Vinnie's game to divert himself from the monotony of the trip to the ferry. Leave the house Vincent, arrive at Demaret Beppo. Some mornings weaving his way down the corridor, going from class to class, waiting for Wendy or the guys, Beppo thought he was alive only those hours he was one of them. When he was back home, he was flying on instruments.

He ran up the subway steps two at a time. He had been worried sick about Wendy. He was a coward, he should have risked their censure and laid a little reality on them. St. Jean's might have requested extra police surveillance; public opinion would force the cops to get tough. Wendy had to stop this before she walked right into a stakeout. The media would turn her deed into the act of a real looney tunes. He couldn't bear that. But he couldn't bear Wendy mocking him either. He dreaded future capers and refused to think about past ones.

Ahead of him, Wendy was at their meeting place, pacing in front of their bench. "Hey, babe, you won the grand prize, *Good Morning America!*" he shouted as he ran toward her.

"Can you believe it! Five weeks, five perfect capers." Wendy was amused by the look of concern on Beppo's face. "You couldn't have thought I'd get caught!"

Wendy was bored performing alone. No audience, no

68

challenge. Last night for a moment she considered screaming *help* or *rape* just to see what would happen. Beppo
couldn't comprehend the magnitude of her sacrifice, performing silently in the shadows. Wendy had nothing to
hide. She was what girls read *Seventeen* to learn.

"But really, Wendybird, it has been a heavy caper.
You've got to stop before the cops —" As he hugged her
close, she could feel his heart pounding right through his
jacket. His fear made the caper worthwhile.

"You know you can pull out anytime we're too much
for you. You don't need our recommendation to get into
MIT." Wendy said, slipping out of his embrace.

"Are you kidding!" He kissed her harder than he ever
had.

As they approached school Wendy was flushed with
pleasure. Underneath his wizard brain, whatever drove
Beppo to audit Sam Goldman's classes, he had common
itchy crotch. She cupped her hand over his ass and waited
for him to open the front door to Demaret. "Is patience a
virtue, Beppo?"

WMNM *Afternoon Talk Show*, "Homer on the Range":

"You're listening to WMNM, this is Carrie Homer, waiting to talk to you! Join our electronic coffee klatch. Hello, Girl, you're on the air!"

"Yeah, hello. First I want to say I listen to your show every day, and I like it very much. About that kid got crushed under the subway train, it don't surprise me. Not one bit. I'm sixty years old and I lived my whole life three blocks from that Ninety-sixth Street station. You know the reason the cops call it an accident is that they don't want to investigate. I bet she was pushed, and I know exactly who did it. There's this crazy nut I noticed many times on that platform, mutters swear words to me even if I walk by and don't even look his way. He pushes his junk in a baby carriage, well I told the token lady he was crazy they should get him out of there before he kills somebody, and now it's too late. If the cops weren't so lazy they'd go find this nut, curses himself too, and shakes his fist at the train, you know what I'm sayin', he's got nothin' to lose, nowhere to go. He probably shoved her off the platform with that baby carriage he pushes, piled with dirty comic books, oh yes, I looked in it one time, to make sure there weren't no baby under all the junk that might need protection, you know? Well he's the one did it. Like a gorilla ape dressed in clothes, does anyone care?"

5

Why don't we spend the day with Kate tomorrow? We'll go to a matinee, my treat!" Wendy studied Elizabeth for her reaction to this novel suggestion.

Elizabeth frowned. "Is this your oblique way of performing penance?"

"I confess. I confess." Wendy danced a few steps ahead of Elizabeth, causing a couple of people to stare at them. "I'm setting the example for the rest of you by admitting my own weakness. I twitted you awfully hard yesterday when I came into the bedroom and found Beppo asleep on your bed, and I'm sorry, sorry, sorry. There! I said it."

Elizabeth nodded in agreement. "I've told you at least a hundred times that Beppo has been hanging out at our house solely for Sam, never for me."

"I know, I know, I jumped to idiotic conclusions."

Elizabeth held up her hand. "Don't compound the felony by saying how impossible it would be for Beppo to be sleeping in my bed for more personal reasons."

Elizabeth looked uncomfortable. "We might be destroying our closeness with these penances all the time. Someone may decide it's easier to keep a secret than go through the routine of confession and thinking up a suitable penance."

Elizabeth suspected that Wendy still thrilled to the words of the Church, even if she had abandoned its ritual. The year Wendy had been a devout Catholic she'd been easier to live with. But after the Church had lost its power over her, her restless energy had returned.

"I think it's fun. Let the punishment fit the crime, and all that. You're always predicting disaster, Lizard. I said I was sorry and I feel so much better for having said it, which is proof our method works." Wendy tossed her head until her hair fell smoothly down her back. "You hiding a dark and delicious secret?"

"Me? What secret could I possibly have?"

Wendy pointed up at the cloudless summery sky. "What's the big deal up there tonight? Beppo didn't have time to explain it."

"Today is July twenty-eighth. Part of our nearest star cluster — Ursa Major — will be visible tonight. Beppo is stupified — he's going to help Sam calibrate the big dish, the telescope, and take some special kind of radio photographs."

"As though Sam couldn't recognize the Big Dipper without Beppo!"

"Don't be too hard on Beppo. Sam's irresistible, especially about his starry sky. That's why Beppo conked out on my bed yesterday. He's been working his butt off, plus traveling two hours home in the wee hours of the morning. He's spending the night with Sam in the lab tonight. Wish you could have heard Sam talking to Mrs. Santini on the phone. Screaming as though it was a remote hook-up to Sicily."

The girls stopped at the corner. Elizabeth rested her canvas bag on the mailbox. "Hello, Mrs. Santini, this is Sam Goldman. I for-got to tell Vin-cent that he should plan to stay over the night at our house. There may be a cloud cover, you see —' Then Tessa jumps in: 'Christ, Sam, she doesn't need a course in astronomy, simply tell her we'll feed the boy cereal in the morning and we'll make sure he brushes his teeth."

"Boy, I'd love to get a peek at Beppo's parents. The whole family for that matter. Think they're right off the boat, the way Beppo describes them?"

"If Beppo is even half as accurate a storyteller as Peter is, then his mother is as much of a pain in the tail as Lenore." Elizabeth pushed the damp hair off her forehead. "I wonder if those people will ever come back. Sometimes I forget that Peter even has parents."

Wendy shaded her eyes from the sun. "Wouldn't I just love Curtis to make good his promises to take Mother to the south of France for the summer. But he's torn between following his own pleasure and policing my every move."

Elizabeth smiled faintly. "Know what I bet? Nirvana to Mrs. Beppo is probably seven sons and seventeen grandsons, all living at home letting Mama wait on them."

"Why do you change the subject every time I mention Curtis?"

"Because you do it with such venom. It's out of proportion."

"*You* live with him," replied Wendy, making an audible effort to keep her tone light. "Think Beppo will ever let us meet the clan?"

"Not a chance," Elizabeth answered immediately. "Who would he be, Mama's Vincent, our Beppo, or Professor Sam's Starshine?"

"You don't like him, do you?"

"He's not one of us; he's studying us."

"At least he had the judgment to pick us," Wendy smiled slyly.

"I'd better make tracks home, Wendy. It's not fair, my coming home every day after Kate has done all the chores on Tess's list."

Chores didn't seem to create a contest between KC and Tess the way they did for Elizabeth and her mother. When Tess told Elizabeth to wash the clothes and clean the oven before she went to Peter's house, Elizabeth saw the task as a measure of Tess's anger with her. Kate often vacuumed the house without being asked, which Elizabeth took as her cousin's way of proving herself irreplaceable in Tess's galaxy.

"Be sure and tell KC that she can pick any show she wants. Lunch, matinee, maybe even a chocolate soda afterward, because I want us all to be friends, *la de dah*." To Wendy, Elizabeth hunched over her bookbag looked like a big cozy dog. "I love you," she said impetuously, tugging lightly at Elizabeth's braid.

"What brought this on?"

"I am you. I am Crunch. I am all of us."

"You are off the wall."

74

"I am filled with love. I am not scarred by years of my father's hate," Wendy answered dreamily.

They walked a block in silence. Elizabeth had always been a bit unnerved by Mr. Tippett, his glad-handing charm such a transparent cover for a me-first-you-a-distant-second view of the world.

"Look out, hurry!" Elizabeth screamed. "Get off the curb, hey kid, move!" She ran down the street.

Wendy followed yelling, "My God, a bus. Watch out, kid, you'll be flattened."

Huddled on the curb, unconcerned about the traffic speeding a few inches from him, a young child was playing with miniature cars. He did not look up at the two girls running toward him. He didn't flinch when the bus driver honked repeatedly, waiting to slide into the curb. Wendy grabbed the boy's shoulder and Elizabeth held up her hands to the bus driver. The boy looked at them without expression.

"You can't play here, that bus might have crushed you." Wendy tossed her bag to the curb and touched his trouser leg.

"He's *wet*, Lizard. His pants are soaking wet!"

The child said nothing, but began to slap his cheek with his fingertips. They stooped, one on each side of him, and continued talking, but he showed no reaction.

"From the aroma, no doubt what it is," Elizabeth grimaced. "Look at his head. His hair is matted. His face is streaked white."

"Gross!" Wendy whispered above his bobbing head.

Elizabeth picked him up under the arms and dragged

him away from the curb, the heels of his sneakers bumping over the pavement. "Tear tracks. Clearly, he's been abused."

The boy's hands lay quietly in his lap. He stared unblinking at Wendy. Unnerved, she turned away, lifting her face to the sun.

Elizabeth bunched up the sleeve of her sweater and wiped the child's face. "What's your name? I'm Elizabeth, she's Wendy."

He didn't answer. A puddle formed around him on the sidewalk: Wendy backed away to avoid the stream flowing toward the curb.

"He's a savage," she said, swallowing hard.

Elizabeth cupped the boy's chin in her hand. "Would you like us to find your mom?"

He didn't respond. Elizabeth wiped his face again but he pulled away and in one springing motion got to his feet. "I want ice cream," he said distinctly. His trousers were marbled; they clung to his legs.

"He can talk," Elizabeth said uncertainly. If he had been deaf, a mute, scarred in some way she could understand, she would have felt easier. She rubbed his thin arms and put her arm around his shoulders. "We are going to take care of you," she said decisively, trying to ignore his gutteral noises.

Wendy picked up her pocketbook, shifted it to her right shoulder and sighed. "Come on, kiddo, he's a loon."

Still the boy did not move.

"He can't react because he's been *beaten*," Elizabeth growled.

76

"What do you suggest we do? We can't take him any place," Wendy whispered out of the side of her mouth. "What would we say, we'd like three Cokes and a box of Pampers?"

"We'll take him to my house." Elizabeth bent to the boy's face. "Would you like to come home with me?"

"I want ice cream."

"What about we call a cop?"

Elizabeth set her mouth firmly and smoothed the hair lying on the boy's forehead. The child jerked away from her and resumed slapping himself, this time on his left eyelid.

"This is swell. We'll be accused of drugging the kid into this state." Wendy stamped her foot. "Don't touch him, Elizabeth, he's probably contagious."

"We can't expect him to trust us right off."

"I need ice cream."

"You think his mother is going to say gee officer, thanks for bringing him home?"

Wendy's coarse tone angered Elizabeth. She arched herself over the small body. "Suit yourself, I'm not afraid of the consequences."

"Get serious, Elizabeth. Your mother will have a fit the instant the kid pees on her upholstery."

"Ice cream!"

Elizabeth had forgotten Tess. "OK, that's a good point. Besides this is Sam's big night. They'll be all involved with the star business. So we'll take him to Peter's. Maybe the boys can convince you helping him is not a sin." Elizabeth gripped the boy's hand and tried to imagine what he'd look like clean.

77

Wendy narrowed her eyelids. "Did you forget it's my week starting today?"

Elizabeth tossed her head and went into the street to hail a cab. The child stood up. Elizabeth's sweater fell below his knees. He was small, his body younger than his weary face.

"I'd like to kill his mother," Elizabeth muttered to Wendy once they were settled in the cab. "Some sleaze bag, that's for sure. Probably doesn't even know he's gone."

"Wrong! She probably told him to go out and play, *encouraged* him even." Wendy wouldn't admit it, but she was impressed with Elizabeth's resolve. Even if they ditched the kid in an hour, it would make one hell of a headline. Boy disappears from Broadway and 110th Street. She knew better than to say that to Elizabeth in her current frame of mind.

Peter gazed fascinated at the boy's hands, clenched like claws, flicking at his cheeks. The boy was docile; he let them take off his shirt and pants.

Objections streamed from Wendy. "Suppose he has a disease; what if he hits his head on the bathtub and dies. He might scream, the cops will be on our backs, and we'll be in grade-A trouble. He's not worth the risk."

"Sounds like you're losing your coolth," Peter observed. "Where's your adventurous spirit, Queen of the Many Capers?"

"You play dolls with him. I'm cutting out."

Wendy was oblivious to the hot summer rain hissing all around her. Running in and out of traffic she gagged on a burst of fumes expelled from the rear of a bus. How could Elizabeth touch that filthy, scabby child?

Breathing hard, Wendy stopped under a canopy. A pink and orange neon sign flashed with floral brilliance. PIZZA PASTA. Raindrops glinted pink and orange as they slid down the glass; a handwritten sign warned no change for the bus, no telephone on premises.

A man in a dark shirt hurried past her to take shelter under the fish market canopy. He had an elliptical bald spot. "Daddy!" she cried. The man turned at the sound of her voice. He was a stranger with a long dark scar on his left cheek. Wendy stared straight ahead to avoid his questioning gaze. She hailed a cab, suddenly anxious to get home. That ditsy kid had really got to her. She longed for her mother's spotless kitchen. For all his devilish rules her father would never have lost her, let her wander alone when she was that kid's age. Curtis had never made her so crazy she'd sit in a puddle of her own pee.

At eight o'clock after watching half a vintage gangster movie, the boy told Peter his name was Dougle Worth. In his slurred singsong voice it sounded at first like *Dooo Wur*. Elizabeth was in the kitchen scooping ice cream into cereal bowls. She had just finished bathing the child. She'd been surprised by the firmness of the boy's chest and stomach. His ribs were distinct ridges; his knees and elbows scabby, his feet so calloused they might have been carved from dark wood.

She tried to look jolly; she laughed and laughed until her face ached. She so wanted him to trust her, tell her his name, confide something which would prove she was

79

more adept at handling him than Peter was. She tried to ignore the way the boy fiddled with his penis as though it were a toy.

Elizabeth had hugged him while she was drying him in a cocoon of towels. "You're not a bit like I was, my friend." She'd been so timid, some days she'd felt she'd burst with dread. Carrying a cup of coffee to Sam she would hear the china smash and feel the hot liquid scald her skin and stain Tess's rug, as vivid as if it had actually happened. She anticipated an encyclopedia of disasters. Some people must have slipped on the soap in the tub or people would never mention it. Poking a knife in a toaster was certain death. She held three fingers against her neck while Tess was knotting her winter scarf just in case Tess pulled it too tight. "Somehow I'll find the key, make you stop this business," she whispered to the child. "I won't desert you the way everyone else has." She was unable to read his blank stare.

Peter's voice interrupted her thoughts. "Lizard, this is Dougle Worth." The boy reached for the bowl of ice cream and spooned it up in greedy mouthfuls. "Cookies," he growled to Elizabeth.

"Today started Wendy's week, right? We'll have to get her back here. We can't keep the kid in towels all night."

"Notice how she shot out of here?" Elizabeth was unable to calm her internal commotion. "Who the hell is she, Miss All Dressed in White?"

"Slow down," Peter said mildly. He put Dougle on the floor. The boy was wearing an old shirt of Benny's that reached below his knees.

"Broken things have no place in Wendy's world."

80

"Plenty of time to worry about Wendy's motives after we dispose of the kid."

"Dispose of him? Like a paper towel?"

"Cool it, Lizard. Who got us into this bind?"

"More ice cream. Coke."

Elizabeth rested her head on Peter's chest, but her trembling hands revealed her nervousness. He rubbed her back but she did not relax.

"Do you miss Lenore?" Elizabeth made vague gestures encompassing the room.

"About as much as you would miss Tess."

"Do you ever resent us for using your apartment and then going home to our parents?"

He smiled in a superior fashion. "You want me to say yes."

"I want ice cream."

Peter was touched by Elizabeth's look of concern for him. "We get along better station to station, believe me, Lizard."

"Tess wouldn't miss me."

"And you want her to," Peter hugged her. "You're not so tough." He entwined his fingers in the soft hair straggling out of her braid. Her face was strained, squinted, as though avoiding a strong light. He pressed his lips to her hair. She'd never connect him with Gina, that was clear. Elizabeth got her sex from books; the Wife of Bath, Moll Flanders were all she knew. And her new crush, Flaubert's spoiled Emma Bovary. For an instant her naïveté excited him. He pulled her close and bent to her lips.

Elizabeth ducked her head and ran from the room, her face burning. She sat on Peter's bed, trying to imagine them together, but she did not have a clue about the mechanics of the thing. If it had gone further, she'd have collapsed on the bed, lying in total ignorance, white and appealing as a boiled pike.

"Here you are." Peter stood in the doorway, her awkwardness forgotten. "Wendy's on her way back here, but she's not happy about it. Matter of fact she sounds mean as a snake. Funny thing is if you'd found the kid yesterday, when it was still your week, it all might have turned out differently. Where is the little charmer anyway?"

She shrugged. "We'd better find him." Elizabeth went into the Zeisses' bedroom. Sheets and blankets dragged on the floor. There was a pile of books on the bedside table, a towel on the floor, a pair of jeans knotted in a figure eight on the faded Oriental rug. Peter must be sleeping in here. What right did Benny and Lenore have to desert him and run off? Middle-aged hippies! She opened the closet door. Dougle was crouched under a rack of plastic garment bags.

"Oh no! No! Dougle, come out here!" She forced herself to stand very still. He would not look at her, but he had not taken up the slapping routine. "Peter, catch him, he's coming out of your parents' room!"

Peter appeared, holding a struggling Dougle. "What's the problem?" Elizabeth pointed to the floor of the closet. In one motion Peter had transferred Dougle to his other hand and was about to smack his behind.

"Stop, Peter, for God's sake. How do you think he got this way?"

"We'll reason with him after he's cleaned up this mess."

Dougle moaned low, continuously. Peter turned to Elizabeth. "Would you get some paper towels for our friend here?"

Dougle continued to moan and did not move to clean up the mess. Peter sat next to him and began to moan. Elizabeth sat on the other side of him, moaning. After looking frantically from one to the other, Dougle bent down and scooped up the mess. Slowly they all moved toward the bathroom.

Elizabeth went into the hall to wait for Wendy. She took the pencil from behind her ear and sketched five odd-shaped stones. Five as one. Resting her cheek against the cool yellow stucco wall, she tried to quash the violent surge of love she felt for Dougle. How could one person become so solitary, so fearless of the "big people" as to continually wet his pants? It had never occurred to her to refuse to read before any of the other kids. She had tried to be good. Dougle had refused to play.

The elevator door opened and Wendy rushed out. "You are acting like a class-A jerk. I don't blame Peter, he marches to the loudest tune. I called Crunch. Unfortunately he insists on bringing Kate."

"We may be Dougle's last chance," Elizabeth said quietly.

Peter was lying on his stomach next to Dougle, watching TV. He rolled closer to Dougle, encircling his rigid body with his arm. Dougle did not take his eyes off the screen, but he raised his hand to Peter's shoulder.

"Remember me, Dougle? I'm Wendy." Elizabeth turned away. Wendy sounded like a movie queen condescending to a ragged fan.

83

"Wendy, would you call Tess? Tell her I'm staying at your house over night — no, say your father will put me in a cab later. If I call, she'll grill me about where I've been, why haven't I called. Especially with Sam at the lab all night, she'll want me home now."

Feeling as dumb and inarticulate as a large animal, Elizabeth lumbered out of the room.

"Glad it's your week," Peter said as soon as Elizabeth was out of earshot. "I couldn't convince her to ditch the kid. It's been a swell couple of hours," Peter rolled his eyes.

"Why the smirk? There's nothing funny here."

"I wasn't laughing, Wendybird. Sisterhood is powerful, right on."

"Dougle's the issue, got it?" Wendy was standing directly under the chandelier, the light turning her hair silvery. "And this pig sty!"

"No reason to turn killer," said Peter sullenly.

Wendy shook her head impatiently, as if a fly were buzzing around her. For an instant she'd seen Peter's apartment through her father's eyes. Dirty glasses on every table, beer cans overflowing the garbage, life out of control. "The kid's getting us all frazzled," she said, a tone of sadness in her voice. "Soon as we get rid of him, we'll be us again."

Elizabeth stood in the doorway, watching them. She had to shake loose of this kid. Item: twelve hours ago she didn't know this kid existed; item: she shouldn't risk even a molecule of the group's esteem for this unknown kid; item: the kid didn't give a damn.

"Guess I've been acting super sentimental," she said

to Wendy. It would be worse to admit she hadn't been acting.

"I've had enough of you and Captain Peter, the kiddie's delight, that's for sure."

Dougle stood up and walked toward Wendy and circled her a few times. His circles became smaller and smaller until he had reduced the space between them to a few inches. He sucked his fingers noisily and looked at her without expression. "Get him ready to leave," Wendy said loudly. "Now!"

Elizabeth made a visible effort to react casually. "Is he ready?"

"His clothes will be out of the dryer in a few minutes."

Kate and Crunch entered the room with the apologetic smiles of late arrivals at a party. Wendy thought they looked awfully cozy, sitting hip to hip. The sooner Wendy put a cork on the entire evening the happier she'd be. Crunch was spending too much time with Kate. That was going to end.

Wendy stood up and shook her hair down her back. "Let's get into action, guys. Call missing persons, they must have a child bureau." None of them moved.

"If you mention some of the kid's habits, they'll advise us to hook up with the sanitation department," said Crunch. He stretched his arm across Kate's shoulders. Then catching sight of Wendy's daggerlike look, he moved a few inches away. Those looks of Wendy's intimidated Kate although she was amused by them too. She reached up and squeezed his hand.

Wendy leaned toward Crunch. "Did you think up that hilarity all alone, my dear?" she asked him coldly. He took his arm away from Kate and sat up straighter.

Elizabeth snatched the phonebook from the shelf. "Before we notify the FBI or the funny farm, what about Worth, N., at 750 Riverside Drive?"

"Worth, N., is worth everything," said Crunch, glad to have something to crow about. "We now take our mobile unit to the home of Worth, N., where our distraught mother will express profound regret at being reunited with her son."

"Crunch! You have as much compassion as a scorpion," Kate said heatedly. "How can all of you sit around and discuss the child as though it were a debate on public TV? He's right here. He has feelings."

None of them answered her.

Elizabeth reached down for her left foot and placed it on her right thigh. "Since I was the one to get involved, it's up to me to get us outvolved." She grinned to indicate mellow spirits.

"I'll go with you," Kate said without hesitation. Maybe Elizabeth's crust was softening.

Crunch frowned at Kate. She had to learn to avoid endangering alliances. Elizabeth was clearly not top dog tonight. If only Kate could be like Gina, happy as ginger ale.

"We'd better get moving then," Wendy said, "before we all rate prime-time appearances as felons on the late news."

Elizabeth cast a sideways glance at Wendy. "Isn't the child more important than our own convenience? We can't sit out every game."

"If you want to Joan of Arc it for the kid, you'll do it

alone." Wendy looked at Peter and Crunch for confirmation.

"I'm not getting involved," Peter said without hesitation.

"Agreed."

Elizabeth sighed. "Agreed."

Wendy smoothed the wrinkles in her jeans. "I'll ride shotgun."

"No need. Kate offered to come with me."

Within sight of the group, Elizabeth was plotting with an outsider. She avoided Wendy's angry squint. *Just this once, there's no time to reason with them; I understand Dougle, and I am right.* Odd, but she felt grateful to her cousin as she met Kate's honest uncomplicated gaze.

Surprised that Elizabeth would choose her over Wendy, Kate jumped up. "Love to, no problem." Immediately she regretted her hearty tone. No matter how hard she tried to fit in with Elizabeth and her friends, Kate couldn't erase her eagerness, the worst of sins.

In the hall Elizabeth whispered to Kate, "I'll need you for about an hour. Then go home and tell Tess I'm spending the night at Wendy's. Since Sam's at the lab, she may already be in bed. Don't wake her. Wait 'til breakfast, and then — be vague about my plans for the day, but not so garbled that she decides to call Wendy. Think you can handle it?"

Kate drew back from Elizabeth's imperious tone.

"I'll call tomorrow and tell her I'm spending the night at Wendy's again. I'll handle her then. You'll be off the hook as soon as I call tomorrow. Don't act *nervous* or Tess will get suspicious. That's the key here."

Kate would have liked to scream at Elizabeth to stop talking as though she were a mental defective. Her parents' death had forced her to survive in Elizabeth's world, acceding to Elizabeth's demands, keeping a low profile around Wendy, whose sly friendliness didn't fool Kate for a minute. Lord, even Crunch studied Wendy's face, looking for clues. He was never totally free of his friends.

Kate sighed. All the emotions careening wildly around the Zeisses' apartment baffled her, tired her. What the hell. If she succeeded at this little task, maybe then Elizabeth would stop glaring at Kate as though she were taking the bread out of her mouth. Looking at the stubborn set to Elizabeth's shoulders, Kate was puzzled. When had her shy cousin become such a powerhouse? As a child she'd been afraid of the ocean, night, dead fish washed up on shore, sitting in the front seat of the car. All those summers sharing the old green cabin on Cape Ann! Kate's mother insisted she be nice to Elizabeth: "Don't you dare call Elizabeth a ninny, a coward, a wimp. She's your cousin!" As though that meant anything.

They walked toward the river, Dougle between them, Kate was touched to see how tenderly Elizabeth held the little boy's hand and smoothed his shirt across his narrow back. Kate wondered if Elizabeth had once hoped some older person would come to rescue her.

Elizabeth caught Kate watching her and blushed. "I'll find a cheap rooming house, check it out, then come back and get Dougle from you. We'll hide out for a couple of days. Don't look so *scared*. Kate, it's time someone showed this little boy that at least one person in the world cares what happens to him. So for the next couple of days, I'm it. I'm going to show I care about him."

"So that's it," Kate said. "I thought it was something like that."

"What's that supposed to mean?"

"Don't get testy, Elizabeth. Remember *please* that he's somebody's kid."

"Somebody doesn't deserve him."

"What if we get caught?"

"Don't worry, Kate. You, as usual, will come out smelling like a rose."

Hiding out with Dougle for a couple of days was a necessary risk. If she could show him that as he got older he'd be able to live his own way, by his own rules, she would have saved his life. To carry it off smoothly she'd think of it as a caper. Wendy did solo capers every week. It was time to prove Elizabeth could pull alongside Wendy in the nerve department. Maybe that would stop Crunch and Beppo from following Wendy even before Wendy had told them where she was going.

So Elizabeth would be Katy Callahan from Boston. Use Kate's ID, every detail must be accurate. Not for the folks she'd be conning, but so that she could report a caper perfectly executed. She was sure the speed of the group's forgiveness would be in direct proportion to the juiciness of her narrative. In a couple of days, she'd return Dougle to Worth, N., and by then maybe the parents would have had enough of a scare to treat the little guy better. Clearly it was the proper plan. Even Wendy would agree. Elizabeth was changing this boy's life, rather more important than letting Wendy have the last word. An hour later Elizabeth had rented a room.

"Then it's all set, Miss Callahan. What a nice sweater, your mother must have knit that. I have the same pattern, made this skirt, 'bout fifteen years back, and it's held its shape good as the day it was blocked. Most of this fake wool they got now, wouldn't knit no dog's blanket with such junk."

"Ma mama knits hats and mittens for all us kids." The great American slice of Momism routine. Crunch would approve. Wheeeoooo!

"Big families are the nicest. I came to New York when I was a girl young as you, my folks didn't want me to go but I came, worked as a hat trimmer. Now ladies don't buy custom hats."

Touching her fingertips to her brow and sucking her teeth, Miss Artemian led the way. Peering over the old bird's shoulder, Elizabeth saw there'd be barely enough room for her and the unpredictable Dougle. But it would do for a couple of days. Dominating the room was a four-poster of dark wood. A massive bureau stood like a dark brooding animal. Elizabeth's heart quickened, keeping pace with her blossoming story. "There was this small chair with arms amputated at the elbows. I'll never forget the pair of whiskey decanters that she'd made into bedside lamps — their shades were the color of diseased gums!"

"Across the hall is your bathroom . . ." The old crone nattered on. The funnier the story, the faster they'd forgive her. Finally she got the key and muttered something about going to the store for a toothbrush. "I shall return,

Miss Artemian." It was what Wendy would have expected of her.

Running back up the hill she saw Kate struggling with Dougle. Waving her arms wildly she called, "Dougle! It's OK, I'm here, honey."

"None too soon," Kate said. Her T-shirt and jeans were glistening wet in the lamplight.

"Jesus, he really did a job. I'll make it up to you, Kate."

"I don't know why you're doing this. He's one squirrelly kid."

"Exactly! Too many people have settled for labeling him. I'm going to show him he's not too dreadful to be loved. Tomorrow I'll take him to the zoo and he can ride in the pony cart and feed the sea lions. It'll be the turning point for him. Remember to be vague around Tess, and for God's sake, don't breathe a word to Crunch."

Elizabeth forced herself to hold Dougle close in spite of the stench. She tiptoed into the dark building. He was silent, no heavier than a bagful of groceries.

Up in the elevator, tiptoe, tiptoe down the hall. The room marked 6. Dougle perched on the faded brocade chair and watched her.

"Would you like a drink of water?"

"I don't drink water before I go to bed."

"Of course not. How silly of me. I'm going to get a towel." Why couldn't she level with him and say she was getting the shower curtain to protect the furniture from his pee? She balanced on the rim of the bathtub. *Yank* those wretched plastic hooks, *yank, yank!* Suddenly a thumping sound. Dougle! She jumped down, left the shower curtain dangling, and ran back to her room.

A piercing scream. Dougle squatting on the floor.

"*No!* Dougle, do it in the bathroom!" Please God, don't let anyone hear him. She shook Dougle by the shoulders. He ran into the hall, screaming one long piercing note.

A Japanese girl was first in the hall. "A little boy," she cried. Elizabeth fought Dougle until she could clamp her hand over his mouth. "Shut up, you little bastard," she snarled. He broke free of her and pounded one of the closed doors. A wizened old lady appeared and threw a blanket over Dougle.

"I've got the little one," she screamed. The hall was confusion. "Call the cops, she's probably a murderer."

Dougle was howling but Elizabeth couldn't reach him. The hall, lit only by the lamps from the bedrooms, was a muddle of thrashing bodies. The old woman was swatting lumps under the blanket, spittle bubbling from the corners of her mouth. Lights came on. Everyone froze. Elizabeth raised her hand. "It's all a mistake. Sorry for the noise."

Miss Artemian jabbed Elizabeth's arm. "Is that your child? I told you no pets and no children."

Elizabeth was laughing too hard to answer.

"She kidnap small boy," the Japanese girl said.

The old woman pulled her crocheted bedjacket around her and snatched the blanket off Dougle. "Poor child's so scared he soiled himself. Call the cops before she murders all of us in our beds!"

"I knew it was foolish taking in someone without references. Bet her mother didn't knit that sweater neither."

It was time to split. Elizabeth shook off the old bat's

grip. When she grabbed Dougle, he screamed. She shook him violently. "Stop that!" He fell against her. His weight calmed her. How could she be acting like Tess, when all she wanted to do was save the kid, not damage him further.

There was a loud rap at the front door. The Japanese girl covered her face with petal-like hands. As the door was thrown open, another boarder shouted through the narrow opening, "We've got a dangerous criminal in here, if you are the police, let me see your badge." She turned back to the other women. "It might well be her accomplice staging a rescue."

"It's the real police," Miss Artemian told her, "I can see his badge glinting in the light."

Elizabeth watched the scene in a state of shock. Had she really caused such hysteria? She sure had misread the night. This was no Alice-in-Wonderland fantasy with rabbits in waistcoats scuttling by. Elizabeth bent to reassure Dougle that they'd be out of here in a minute as the two policemen burst into the room.

Miss Artemian clutched the cop nearest her. "Terrorist Arabs, that's who sent her. To blow us up, officer, arrest her."

Elizabeth winked at the second cop. "Don't you guys screen the lunatics who scream cop in the night?"

He was intimidated by her, probably took a lot of teasing about his orange hair and freckles. He looked to be about fourteen and had a wide backside.

"Is your gun loaded?" Elizabeth asked in a musical voice.

He opened his spiral notebook. "I'll ask the questions."

"Come here, darling," Elizabeth lifted Dougle onto her lap.

"Name?"

"Mine or his?"

He narrowed his eyes and called to his partner.

"Just fooling, *officer*. I am Emma Bovary."

"Address?"

How long until he winked at her, collected his buddy and wisked her and Dougle out of here. Could she ask them to drop her at Peter's?

"Address, you and the boy?" He leaned closer to her.

"I am no doped-out teenage thrill-seeker," she said coldly. "We both know this is a silly mistake."

"What is your relation to the boy?" he asked tonelessly.

She felt like grabbing his glass gun and smashing it on the floor.

"I am the boy's grandmother." If she could ignore his ridiculous cowlick that sprouted from the center of his head, if only he'd put his cop hat on again. "The child has been abandoned." She touched Dougle's wet jeans. "As you can see, he has a rather unusual concept of personal hygiene."

"You have the right to remain silent —"

"Just like TV. Now I'm getting my money's worth." She squeezed Dougle and held the cop's gaze. Watery eyes, flesh-colored lashes. She glanced furtively at his pad. Angular handwriting. What did any of it matter, so long as he drove her to Peter's.

"Keep wising off, miss. You're going to spend the night

94

in the tank. They said you kidnapped this boy. Hey, Martin, come get this kid."

"No, he'll frighten Dougle." She rose but the cop pushed her back into the chair.

"Lady says she kidnapped him, held a gun on them, can't find the gun, kid was so scared he shit his pants." Martin reached for Dougle. Elizabeth waited for him to bite the cop's wrist, but Dougle tricked her again. He held the man's hand without a struggle, forcing Elizabeth to go back three spaces.

"We can drop him at the shelter, put his description over the air."

Elizabeth stretched, bone tired. She hoped she could stay on top of this thing until they dropped her at Peter's. He and Crunch could handle the cops. She couldn't remember whose week it was; looking at the crude little boy, she thought ruefully, Dougle *who*, what was it she'd been so set on proving?

"Radio for another car, matron for the boy and one for Miss Bovary."

"The burden of proof is on you gentlemen," Elizabeth said, looking at them as though they were shoe salesmen who had failed to find her size in stock. "You can't drag a citizen out of the house in the middle of the night. Don't play me for a moron." She was getting her second wind!

"Isn't your house. Juvenile office downtown will call your parents."

"I assume they tested you before they gave you the weapon and the walkie-talkies. I'm innocent until you clowns prove me guilty." *Clowns* had been a mistake.

Only Wendy could get away with such burning sarcasm. The freckled one shot to his feet, fumbling his notebook in the process, which made him sputter angrily, "You've got their statements. Let's take her downtown." He narrowed his eyes at Elizabeth. "We can hold her 'til the DA proves her guilty."

Elizabeth debated rubbing his nose in his false statements. For the first time all night, she was on the mark factually. But she had mishandled the business so wretchedly, conciliation was no longer possible. She must not show fear. "I'm entitled to one call," her imperious tone had deteriorated to a wobble. She stood up and brushed past Freckles. She stumbled and fell hard. Forgetting her dignity she screamed. "He tripped me purposely. He's no cop!" The boarders crowded around her, the old woman squatting to get a better view. Elizabeth doubled over clutching her stomach. "He kicked me, it's police brutality." Dougle set up a long howl. Elizabeth didn't know if it was for her or against her.

"We'll have the whole building in here. Take the boy and wait for the matron downstairs. I'll follow with Miss Bovary."

"Don't put your hands on me," Elizabeth said viciously. All the years they'd been gliding past parents and teachers without a blemish, and she, first time solo, up against two teenage cops and some decrepit old bats, had bungled it. She was running out of time to set things right. One more try, this time full of goodwill and repentance. "I'm sorry I behaved so stupidly. I guess I'm scared." Neither one answered, but they were listening. "My real name is Elizabeth Goldman, and I live about five blocks uptown. On Riverside Drive."

"Told me her name was Callahan and showed me ID from Boston. I knew something was fishy, but I gave her the benefit of the doubt." Miss Artemian clasped and unclasped her hands. "Mother probably didn't even knit that sweater."

The scene was escalating too quickly for Elizabeth. Would she be able to recreate for Wendy and the boys the anonymous fury of the old woman?

Of course they'd forgive her. A much calmer Elizabeth walked next to the policeman. Standing at the curb, neither of them speaking, they might have been waiting for the uptown bus.

From another door to the building burst the other cop holding Dougle. As they moved underneath a streetlamp Elizabeth could see them struggling.

"You want me to rescue your partner," she said in what she hoped passed for a neutral, even friendly tone.

"Stay where you are."

"Why don't you drop me by my parents' apartment? On the way to the joint of course." She winced as soon as she'd spoken. Life with Tess had not left her fit to ask favors.

"Wouldn't be surprised if they were relieved you're gone," he said as he waved to a woman in a navy suit hurrying toward them.

"That's sure the truth," she said.

"This the kid?" The woman was taller than either of the male cops. Short stiff dyke hair, no waistline, could model as a refrigerator or fire hydrant. Probably wrestles mountain lions on her day off.

"I'm Elizabeth Goldman, and I live at 699 Riverside Drive." Elizabeth held out her hand, delighting in the picture of the woman leaning forward and biting her hand off at the wrist. "She eyed me as though I was made of gingerbread, Crunch." Elizabeth heard them all praising her with laughter.

"Name's either Emma Bovary or Callahan, she's used both tonight."

The police woman stiffened. "Emma Bovary. I see. You drive, Mac, I'll ride in back with the perpetrator." Once settled in the car, door locked, radio blaring commands and static, the woman said, "This is all vastly amusing. Think you'll come out a heroine? 'Boy, were they dumb, they actually believed my name was Emma Bovary,' " the woman taunted in a high-pitched voice. "Well, sweetheart, I've read Flaubert and I'm real impressed."

"I'm sorry, my name is Elizabeth Goldman."

"Why not Emma Goldman?"

"Because my mother has no sense of humor."

It had been a snap to be more clever than Abbott and Costello. Now the sides were even. This bulwark of a woman might even have the advantage. Elizabeth felt laughter forming inside her, terrible nervous laughter. She tucked her chin to her chest so the cop wouldn't see her mouth twisting in an effort to smother puffs of laughter. She had read the most effective method of torture during the Inquisition had been suffocation from tickling. The supreme irony — death by laughter.

Sam would insist it was merely an unfortunate case of bad judgment. Tess would make several swipes at unearthing Elizabeth's motivation. She loved to bump around inside her daughter's head, determined to unveil the *why* of her.

Inside the station house the noise was unbearable. Three rowdy men were yelling and pointing at the floor. Tess had taught her daughter how to behave at the theater or at a hotel, but no one had coached her about protocol at a police station.

Several men were typing, telephones rang, numbers and commands were broadcast over a loudspeaker, an unseen dog barked. At an eruption of robust female laughter behind her, Elizabeth turned. As soon as she moved, her arms were pinned to her sides. She looked at the cop's impassive face. Pitted skin. She had no best feature. She would have made a colorful warden in a low-budget film. The laughter continued. A woman with an enormous mane of dyed red hair sashayed past her. She was wearing a tight turquoise dress and matching boots; stilletto heels clicked on the cement floor; the hair looked lifeless under the fluorescent lights, which cast the familiar shadowless glare of a McDonald's. Several policemen were gathered around the woman, who trailed cheap perfume. One cop twisted a strand of her hair and the woman leaned toward him and tickled his chin. If only I had a scrap of that woman's flash, Elizabeth thought. She's played this scene a lot of times before.

"This way," the cop guided Elizabeth toward the desk, holding firmly to her arm.

"What are they going to do to me?"

"You'll have your chance to make a statement. I suggest you stick to the facts, Miss Goldman."

Elizabeth smiled. She had got through to the woman after all. She suddenly felt affectionate toward this clunky creature who had to spend her time riding around in the back seats of compact cars keeping company with hookers and thieves. She probably hadn't had a case like her and Dougle in her whole career.

"I didn't steal Dougle. I'm not laughing at you, I know this is serious."

"If anyone should be laughing it's me. At the way you kids cover your stupidity with arrogance. You think you're a special case, right? About three times a night special. Oh not peeing kids snatched off the street, but kids who think they got skin made of suede. You'll be a hero in school — cops, station house, funny rules. Guess what? We all gather around the coffee machine at the shift change, around six A.M., and we laugh. We got buddies too."

"You frisk her yet, Jen?"

"Taking her back now. Want to get her statement here or there?"

"Room three is empty. I'll send in a steno."

She moved down the corridor with Elizabeth still in her grip. Cut loose from all familiar surroundings, Elizabeth suddenly felt the enormity of a caper enacted alone. How could she have traded belonging for fleeing nowhere with Dougle?

"You're right," Elizabeth turned to the cop. "I've been stupid, a real jackass," she said fiercely.

"Don't get carried away with confession."

"It never occurred to me that the police would get involved." She thought for a moment. "I've never even spoken, I mean personally, to a policeman, or policewoman, before tonight."

"Who cares?"

"I get to make one call?"

"Soon as you're searched."

"Searched?" Elizabeth glanced at the fly-spotted green walls. Watermarks veined the ceiling. The floor needed waxing. Got to remain calm, Elizabeth shuddered. Room was probably soundproofed. She would rather be worked over unconscious. But she didn't even feel dizzy. The woman's hands were massive. Elizabeth sighed at the thought of this stranger running her fingers down her legs.

The cop shook her head. "I don't get my jollies poking at sullen kids in sweaty T-shirts."

Elizabeth wanted to suggest the woman find another line of work, in more pleasant surroundings. Sometimes, I'm your daughter, Tess.

6

For two days after they had extricated her from the station house, Elizabeth slept. She woke every few hours, drank some ginger ale, which Tess replenished. No one said more than please and thank you, good morning and good night. But on Friday morning when Elizabeth woke, she was anxious to set things right. Face the music time she thought grimly. Clad in a short cotton nightgown, she tiptoed to the kitchen, hoping Tess had left for Lincoln Center. Sam would be much easier to deal with.

"Good morning," Tess's tone indicated it was anything but. "Kate tried to explain what you were doing with somebody's child in a rooming house, but I'd like to hear your version. Maybe it will shed some light on this mess."

"Kate doesn't know her ass from apples."

"Elizabeth! You were arrested! If you had been two years older you would have been charged with kidnapping! You, not Kate, are the problem!"

Elizabeth raised her eyebrows, but she couldn't think of any withering retort.

"Kate has been distraught, worrying about you, tiptoeing around so as not to disturb you. Sam and I decided to call Peter. He sounded mystified. Lord knows what goes on in that place."

Elizabeth stifled a groan. She should have figured Tess would involve as many people as possible in the drama.

"I found this kid when Wendy and I were coming back from Sam's office. They all tried, Peter included, to convince me to take him back to the corner where we found him. But I thought I should try to reach him, to find out what kind of home was so terrible, he'd rather roam the streets. He's only about six or seven."

For a moment Tess looked sympathetic. It was what she would have done herself.

"I don't know what tale Kate told you. She must have given you the expurgated version. Did you sniff her clothes?"

Tess recoiled and tapped her fingernail against the side of the cup.

"Yes, Mother, *pee!* The kid *pees* in the street, in the bed, in the hall, on Persian rugs. Aren't you glad I didn't bring him near your velvet house!"

"Your father misses the most important night of the stellar year. He might as well have been in Peru in some cave for all of Ursa Major he saw. We've got lawyers doing tap dances to ensure you don't get smacked with two years probation. My velvet house? Ha!"

Wordlessly they measured each other. Tess made a visible effort to control herself. Later Elizabeth would wonder why she stayed in the kitchen knowing her tongue made of granite would only incite Tess.

"You think you have hoodwinked the world. You

haven't fooled anyone. You and your cohorts aren't half so special as you think. Sam —"

"— loves his daughter," Elizabeth rasped, fighting back tears.

"You don't know the meaning of love. When have you given us pleasure, lurking in corners, smirking behind your hands. *Look at me when I'm speaking.*" Panting Tess hurled her coffee cup across the room.

The worst of it was that she knew Tess was right. Staring out of her bedroom window, Elizabeth watched the trees separating Riverside Drive from the highway. She imagined the trees gliding on rollers in time with the cars. In a few moments, these cars, streetlamps, road signs, would roll miles away from this window. If only she could disappear with them, magically hidden in the high branches of a horse chestnut tree.

"Well, I'll be blue, if it ain't Ma Barker." Crunch's face was brimming with amusement as he opened the door to the Zeisses' apartment.

"Cut the crap, Crunch."

Beppo smiled at her fitfully. They'd all been furious at Elizabeth for sneaking off with the kid, but none of them was afraid of the cops or even their parents' response. Wendy had made it very clear to them that Elizabeth's punishment would be meted out by the group, not by some *authorities.*

"Where is everybody?"

"Well Peter is getting ready to come to the country with me and Kate and Gina. Wendy is inside, I am here, and you — are in mega-trouble."

Kate ran over to Elizabeth and tried to put her arm around her. "Are you OK? Do you feel all right?"

"Sure," Elizabeth said, embarrassed that her voice had a distinct quaver, her hands were beginning to tremble. "Wendy, can I talk to you privately for a minute?" Elizabeth shoved her trembling hands into her jeans pockets and said in a stage whisper, "Tess is smashing teacups, not a pretty sight."

"You held a secret from us! Don't give me Tess," Wendy said, her voice low and deadly. "We'll wait 'til Monday to discuss it, away from Kate, Gina, and other extras. You have the weekend to come up with a suitable penance."

Elizabeth reached out to touch Wendy's arm. Tess's rage had been steamy; Wendy, whose eyes were the color of concrete, radiated control. "None of us will be swayed by *gestures*," Wendy said softly. "The bottom line is you held a secret, you could have destroyed us."

Walking back up Broadway, Elizabeth returned her attention to the problem of Tess. Sam would be no safe harbor. In some ways, she dreaded his disappointment far more than Tess's rage, which she heard daily, hidden among the whispered syllables of her mother's conversations.

The apartment was deserted; Tess had left no note on the refrigerator. The air smelled of a neighbor's fried dinner. With Kate away for the weekend, there'd be nothing but her and Tess squaring off, going over and over what she'd done 'til it lost all meaning. The gray twilight suited her isolation. She went into Sam's study and sat in his chair. Tilting back, she rested her feet on

the ottoman. Here Sam read late into the night, often falling asleep in his clothes. Since his lab sessions were at
night, he lived a different schedule from Tess and Elizabeth, who left the apartment before eight. She hoped Sam
would get home before Tess. She was feeling sluggish. All
day she had avoided a stinging truth: she didn't care
whether Dougle went back to his parents or was perma-
nently filed away in some children's shelter. He could
spend the next five years carving a spoon into a dagger.
In spite of all their successful capers, Elizabeth felt six
years old herself, surrendering to the fact that the adults
decide what the children will do.

"There you are, baby." Sam dropped his briefcase on
the floor and laid an armload of books on his desk. "Why
are you sitting in the dark?"

He turned on the lamp on his desk. Its base was cherry
wood, which cast a soft pinkish glow. The wood curved
into the axis of a painted globe, its faded lines delineating
Galileo's world.

"How long have you had that lamp?"

"Your mother gave it to me when we got married. Remember how you used to spin the globe when you were
little?"

" 'That lamp cannot be replaced,' Tess'd say, as though
I could be."

"Kids do have funny notions."

Elizabeth squeezed her father's hand. "I'm sorry I made
you miss so much valuable time the other night. I'd forgotten all about Ursa Major, all I was thinking about —
well, it doesn't matter now. It sounds trite, but I mean it,

Daddy, I wish I could take back that whole night."

"Why did you take the boy?"

"He seemed so helpless. Some sentimental intention I had that I was going to show him I cared, and other people would care."

"There is a bright side. The social worker told us Dougle's mother had been worried sick, she's not the wicked witch you thought. He'd wandered away from her in the supermarket. You must have spotted him at the precise moment he escaped."

How like Sam to find out all the details and construct a logical explanation. "Give me a break, Sam. The kid's hair was matted, he pees in the street."

"Honey, this boy has people who care about him. His folks seemed ordinary, we saw them at the police station, while you were still . . . inside." He tried to smile, but his face held a solemn expression.

"Some children really are ditched, though. The sergeant said people give false names, phony addresses. Three or four kids are abandoned every day in New York."

"Damn it, Elizabeth, you can't go around taking people. If this little boy seemed to need help, the intelligent thing would have been to ask Tess what to do."

"Since when have I opted for the right decision?" She kissed the top of his head. "Where is Tess anyway? I owe her a full-scale apology with brass bands — the whole works. I was kind of grisly this morning."

"She's tied up downtown, but I know an apology — not a forced one — would make her feel a lot better about this whole thing." Sam looked immensely relieved. "Tell you what. How about we go out for Chinese — a little fried rice and moo goo gai pan?"

"Super. Could we go to the movies together afterward?"

"I wish I could, but I've got to do a diagram of Messier 31, you remember, the Andromeda Galaxy? Sorry, Dimple, I didn't mean to get off on a tangent."

"You haven't called me Dimple since I was tiny. How did it start anyway?"

"You had hurled a pail at Kate, and she ran across the sand and jammed her shovel into your cheek. The shovel was sharp and you had to have a few stitches. Your mother was distressed that it would leave an ugly scar. So I said it was a dimple."

"Sorry I asked."

A grizzle-bearded drunk wearing torn brown trousers was holding out a bottle of dago red with a three-inch collar of Indian beads, the kind Lenore used to string for his birthday. The man swayed. "You got to ring your thumb cymbals each time one of us takes a swig."

"Why should I follow his rules?" Peter thought. But he pretended to ring the cymbals to humor the old buzzard. After all it was his elevator.

"What floor you want?" he asked the man, who had collapsed on the floor, muttering and chanting into the neck of the bottle.

The light in the elevator was dimming; then a spotlight fell on a hideous wound exposed on the man's left shinbone. Peter snatched the bottle and took a swig. Instantly the bottle turned to glowing heat. The skin fell from Peter's hands like a pair of gloves.

Where the skin had peeled away, Peter saw his bones neatly labeled with their Latin names. Red and blue blood vessels crisscrossed the bones. They were connected to finely spun wires laced into sleek twists of muscle.

"A breakthrough fiber," the guru whispered, "elongates and retraces just like the real thing. Wire similar to pre-laser tech." The man's voice sounded familiar.

The real thing? Peter was confused. "I am the real thing."

The guru cackled and took another slug of wine. The light brightened in the elevator. He had no beard; he was wearing a lab coat now. His torn trousers were spotless. Impervious to the green and yellow wound on his leg, the man smoothed the trousers over his thighs. "You don't know the half of it, kid. Wire wizardry, labs full of scientists searching for secrets, searching for ways to reduplicate what's been there all along."

"Do you know Sam Goldman?" Peter asked him. "Are you Sam Goldman?" he whispered. The light flickered. Peter bent low to examine the man's wound. It was no longer repulsive. "You mean there's circuitry in everybody's arms and legs?"

The guru motioned Peter to come closer. He slit his pants leg open, and rolled up a flap of skin revealing a section of his left thigh. Red and blue cables were thicker than the ones Peter had observed in his own hand. The wires glinted in the fading light. There was a faint scent of burning rubber.

The man held Peter's fingers and gently touched them to each layer of material. "See, no plasmids, no enzymes, very few moving parts, nothing organic here. The real fun is found in the organs." Rolling down the skin — or was it his trouser leg — to cover his thigh, the man shook his head in disgust. "I'm behaving badly. Grandstanding." He pulled a scalpel from his coat pocket. When had he changed to surgeon's greens? "Unbutton your shirt, you'll see chemical information right under your shirt, enough to understand every microorganism in God's universe."

"Don't touch me, the blood will leak out," Peter cried and pounded the wall in terror. "I know that much!" Panic rose inside him — they were going to bleed him dry. His hands looked like the guts of a radio. "Don't cut me open. I can keep your secret."

Peter could see morning light, but he could not slow down the pounding of his heart. How long before the cables in his chest swelled? They might burst through his skin, which the guy had told him was no thicker than the peel of an apple.

Peter jumped out of bed, the dream still imprinted on the air. He ran to the kitchen to tell Lenore that he had finally been touched by the transcendental guru.

The kitchen was dark. He opened the refrigerator. He had forgotten to buy milk yesterday. The heel of the bread was whiskered with mold. He dressed hurriedly. Damn Lenore for living in that blazing desert. He dressed hurriedly, grabbed his overnight bag, and bought a Danish at the corner bakery. By the time he'd eaten half the pastry, the dream had left him. Bursting cables, splendid circuitry? He slowed his pace. He was in no hurry to get to the Maxwells. Going to the country with them for the weekend was merely another way of killing time. Even Gina seemed like a way to kill time.

Hating Saturday for being a balmy blue August day, the sky seemed to float above the trees, perfect weather to be in the country, Elizabeth rehearsed her confrontation with Wendy and the boys. She ate a handful of cookies and went out for a walk. How could she set things right? Face it, Elizabeth, an afternoon of confession beats a month of walking around alone. They were all off in the country, KC sharing a room with Gina, Wendy preferring to punish Elizabeth rather than get away from her parents for the weekend.

"Look out," screamed three kids careening down the path on skateboards. Elizabeth fell onto the grass. They sped past her, laughing and calling her clumsy. She wiped her hands on her T-shirt and studied the building across the street. It bayed out in a quarter of a circle, hugging the corner of 100th Street. 750 *Riverside Drive*.

She got to her feet and ran across the lawn. Running and leaping across the browned off grass, reaching up to touch the branches of the stunted cherry trees she felt graceful. Inside the hall she read the list of names on the doorbells. She held down the button for Worth, N. A muffled voice uttered some phrase rendered indistinguishable by the accompanying static on the intercom. Elizabeth garbled an answer and leaned against the door as the lock was released.

Seventh floor. Squinting in the dim hallway, the only light from a filthy window that fronted on an airshaft, she finally found the correct door. The woman would be justified in calling the police. But Elizabeth dismissed that possibility and rang the bell.

"What do you want?" Elizabeth couldn't see the face that peered out from a slit in the door, which was secured with a chain. The voice was soft and not threatening.

"Please let me talk to you, Mrs. Worth. Don't slam the door, I know you must hate me. I'm Elizabeth Goldman, the girl who — who — took —" Her discomfort was nothing compared with the daring of it all.

The door closed and the chain slid back. The door opened and Elizabeth was shaken for a moment. She was looking at an older version of herself.

"Come in for a moment, but I'll tell you upfront I don't want to make a tea party out of this. Boy, you had me spinning my wheels. He disappeared while I was piling Pepsi into the cart. The manager was a prince. Take it easy, madam. What's the boy's name? Douglas, your mommy is looking for you. Over and over on the loudspeaker. OK, he hands me the loudspeaker, one of those funnel-shaped things we used to use at peace marches. Dougle bug, I shout with all these damn women slowing their carts as they pass by. Nothing. He's not in the store. Once he had hidden in an empty carton near the checkout. Not this time. Of course the manager is thrilled the kid is no longer on his premises. Not his problem any more. 911 says we don't call him *missing* until he's gone twenty-four hours. From the time of the call or the time he disappeared? They hang up on me. The cops say we'll keep an eye out for him. I go home and call the hospital emergency rooms. What was he wearing?" She broke off and coughed.

While the woman had been talking, wringing her hands, her moist brown eyes never looking at Elizabeth, but rather at the walls and ceiling, Elizabeth had heard a constant hammering. She had tried to glimpse over the woman's shoulder to see if Dougle was in the room. But she was cowed by the blast of words.

"Dougle's been bugging me since he got back, he wants a seahorse. What did you kids tell him about seahorses? Never been near the sea, I come from the Midwest, my husband too, and all our vacations, and they are precious few, are to my folks or his in southern Illinois."

"He's a marvelous child."

"He's a screwed up mess."

"Is he here?"

"Don't you hear him? No need to look embarrassed. I've entertained case workers, psychologists, school aides — all given a license to pry and distort people's lives because they've passed some half-assed course at Hunter. 'Your son should be interacting with his peers. It says so on this graph. Come to our office in three days when we will have evaluated you and your child. The interfacing between home and school is critical to his development. By the way, he can't come to school 'til he stops his anti-social behavior.' "

"I hate social workers as much as you do," Elizabeth said fiercely.

"You ever meet one?"

"No."

"What you want to know is how come Dougle pees on the street. Is his mother a user, an abuser, maybe a sadistic hooker?"

Elizabeth laughed to cover her acute embarrassment. This was not working out the way she'd planned. She'd expected Mrs. Worth to be as squirrelly as that rooming-house freak. "We never thought such things."

"You took him to bug your parents?"

"He seemed alone, you see he was crying so pitiously —"

"No way. Dougle doesn't cry. It's part of his syndrome."

Mrs. Worth motioned to Elizabeth to follow her. "Long as you're here, might as well have a cup of coffee. So you want Dougle to be abused, to make what you did noble instead of stupid."

Elizabeth shook her head, unnerved at the hard tone in the woman's voice. She was so pale, tired, her shoulders sloped, her hair hung in long strings. What shamed Elizabeth the most was that she did not have that in-charge toughness Tess had. She could push against her mother time and time again — and Tess would never topple. This hapless woman needed someone to protect her. Her husband had probably abandoned her and Dougle years ago. Maybe that's why he was so weird.

"I want to apologize to you," Elizabeth lowered her voice and struggled against the urge to ask why she didn't accept help from a social worker or welfare agency, why didn't she do something? *Don't settle,* she wanted to shout. Tess would have reeled off telephone numbers of people downtown, the mayor, a congressman. She'd know how to win the woman's confidence. "Could I say hello to Dougle?"

"Dougle, come see who's here to see you," she screamed over her shoulder. "Why did you flinch? Don't people holler where you come from? Sorry, but he keeps the television so loud, he couldn't hear a helicopter if it landed on the roof outside his window." She talked in spurts. She might be on speed. Elizabeth was glad the group didn't know what a mess the woman was. Clearly no one they'd respect her for tangling with.

Dougle's face appeared from around the corner. When he saw it was Elizabeth, he came into the room and asked her if she'd brought him a seahorse. She shook her head and reached out to pat his shoulder. He was wearing a torn gray T-shirt with Bugs Bunny chewing a carrot on the back. Dougle couldn't even wear a T-shirt the normal way.

To avoid her touch, Dougle twirled away from her, squatting then jumping. His complex set of movements tripped him and he fell, hitting his head on the floor with a loud crack. In an instant his mother reached him and swung him high into the air. With a graceful dip she settled him on her right hip. She's used to him, Elizabeth thought, she knows all his moves. He rubbed his head but he didn't cry.

"I didn't promise him a seahorse," Elizabeth said nervously. "I would never lie to a child. It's the most contemptible thing in the world."

"Is it?"

"Children can't defend themselves," Elizabeth shot

back, then blushed. The woman might take it as an accusation.

Dougle drifted out of the room. He's really on another planet, Elizabeth thought.

Mrs. Worth sighed and put the coffee cups in the sink. "The current shrink's game plan is to lock him in the john until he *performs,* he's looking for a strong parental figure. He's testing me, he says. Of course the wizard doesn't say what I should do, all the time on guard trying to catch him in the act. I feel guilty if I want to meet a friend for lunch. Because that's the day we might get the breakthrough. The school won't let him come back 'til he's cured. Just be firm says Dr. Seventy Dollars an Hour."

"He's diagnosed Dougle?" Elizabeth hesitated. This woman had an edge to her words, sharp as broken glass.

"He's diagnosed Dougle and he's diagnosed me. Dougle's got an expensive problem and we have the money to pay for it." Mrs. Worth took Elizabeth by the hand and led her to the living room. "Look!"

Unable to continue her nonchalance, Elizabeth walked around the room. Bare wood floors, a card table with three bridge chairs around it. On the floor some pieces of a jigsaw puzzle. One upholstered chair and footrest had a shower curtain draped across them. Chintz floral drapes hung to the windowsills. A few plants straggled from their macramé holders in front of the windows. "Stripped for action, huh?

"I can't have people for dinner, the furniture's being reupholstered —" She paused, her fingers drumming on the door frame.

Elizabeth longed to leave. She had no place here, but her pride would not allow her to flee. She owed Dougle that much. "Has he always been — did he ever —"

"Was he toilet trained?" she asked, becoming agitated. "I'm not one to brag," she waved her arms. "But this little guy was perfect, dry all night, never an accident, by his third birthday he was *dripless*. I guess it was too easy." She walked slowly around the room, touching the back of each folding chair.

Elizabeth looked away. "When did this happen?"

"Second week of kindergarten, super-bright kid, accelerated class, he could *read* before he went to school!"

Elizabeth's stomach felt as though the woman had reached over and squeezed it. All mothers claimed super powers for their kids. They were hurried through karma, trained to follow opera scores, fluffed, stuffed. She couldn't remember a time when she hadn't wanted to be best. "When did it all turn sour?" she wondered.

"Sorry we couldn't be more help." Dougle's mother stood in the hallway gently rubbing her son's back until the elevator came.

7

f you went to bed at a proper hour, you'd be able to get up in the morning." Wendy did not open her eyes although she felt her father's breath on her arm. One Sunday she'd love to wake up peacefully. By the time they arrived at church *love* was the last word Wendy'd use to describe her feelings. The love of her father was fierce, eruptive. Nothing like the sweet sad smile on the face of the tender shepherd of men that hung in every church school classroom. Curtis knew a different Christ. The one Curtis evoked each evening as he offered thanks before dinner was more a business consultant, a colleague, than the Lord of Lords. It would be impossible for her father to recognize any power greater than his own.

"You'd better get up now!" Curtis touched his daughter's foot under the bedcovers.

"It's only seven-thirty. We are going to eleven o'clock," her voice shook. She moved her legs to the furthest corner of the bed. "Why can't I sleep late one morning a week? It's not a sin, you know."

"Discipline, my girl. Without it you're nothing in this

world. And don't you forget it. You and your sullen friends, lounging around the Zeisses' apartment doing God knows what. Discipline, that's what all you kids need."

Wendy closed her eyes. A few minutes later she heard her father bellowing at her mother. "You do this to me every Goddam Sunday. Just once I'd like to see you and your daughter up and moving about on your own. I have to do the thinking for everybody in this house."

A few minutes later he was back at the doorway to Wendy's room. She knew he'd come back. So she'd held herself in exactly the same position he'd left her in. "That's why I insisted you stay in town this weekend, my girl. Discipline! At least when you're home I can be sure you're supervised. The Maxwells don't come to church unless the weather's too foul to go to the country. All the dough in the world for their own pleasures, but no money for the work of the Lord." He laughed sharply.

Wendy could no longer hear him. A roar in her ears insulated her from her father's words. She kicked off her covers, a poor substitute for what she really wanted to do to him. She dressed with no pleasure. When she was going to school, or meeting Beppo at the subway entrance, she watched herself in the mirror as she slipped on her bra, her panties, smoothed the folds of a silk shirt close to her skin. But on mornings like this one when she had been snared in her father's Sunday, she didn't even glance in the mirror.

On her way to the kitchen about an hour later, Wendy passed her father without a word. He was spraying Binaca, preparing his mouth to receive the Host. Hallelujah!

Wendy muttered under her breath. Elizabeth would pay dearly for breaking the back of Wendy's Sunday.

Wendy was pouring herself a large glass of orange juice when her mother hurried into the kitchen, fastening a bracelet. "What time is it, darling?"

"Possibly about ten o'clock. But ask Big Ben out in the hall. He's been tolling the time for the last two hours."

Lily Tippett ran across the room and flung open the wall oven as though she were freeing a prisoner. "Wendy, if the roast weighs seven pounds, almost eight —"

"Two hours and eighteen minutes if you want it to be running the Blood of the Lamb."

"Wendy! I forbid you to spout such blasphemy." Lily's pale face had pinkened with rage.

Wendy'd almost given up trying to get her mother to see the light. How many afternoons had she come home from Demaret to find her mother cooking, pots bubbling on the stove, bowls filled with gourmet mixtures that would be cooked to perfection for Curtis's guests? He was as proud of his wife as he was vain about his Rolls-Royce, his genuine Impressionist painting, his condo in St. Maarten. He bragged about Lily's expertise in the kitchen to everyone they met, but only the chosen few were invited to the Tippett's intimate dinner parties.

At these dinners, Curtis acknowledged his wife almost as frequently as he bragged about his rapport with the Lord. Wendy was revolted watching guests sample her mother's salmon mousse and gateau genoise. Wouldn't catch Tess Goldman devoting her life to fluting crusts and whisking sauces. Why couldn't her mother buy a cake at a fancy bakery and pass it off as her own?

Occasionally Wendy would break her vow of silence and confront her mother directly. "You're a person in your own right — you don't need to work like a common laborer for him. Why don't you hire a cook if gourmet meals are so all-fire important?"

"If you're lucky, you'll get a man half as good as your father." Lily set her cookbook in its lucite holder.

Wendy bowed her head with the guests. She kept her eyes open to watch the familiar spectacle. Curtis took Lily's hand and lifted his gaze to the chandelier as though a prayer hung from each pear-shaped crystal. For as long as Wendy could remember, he had been delivering the same improvised blessing in that oily voice, ingratiating himself with God, planning ahead like a smart executive. Wendy knew as soon as the guests murmured amen, Curtis would kiss Lily's hand and shrug off his prayer. He would call it his one-on-one with the Almighty. The guests' approval would linger in the air. They'd wish they could chat so easily with Jesus.

The odor of the steaming meat made Wendy queasy. She averted her eyes as her father slowly drew the newly sharpened blade of the carving knife through the roast. Wendy was disgusted with her mother's intensity, carefully following Curtis's movements so that she would have a spoonful of ratatouille ready when he handed her the next plate. O boy, is Elizabeth going to pay for this, Wendy thought, twisting her napkin in her lap. My kingdom come, my will be done.

"Keep that plate, Wendy, I gave you well-done slices." Curtis's face looked juicy. Wendy imagined that his jacket hanging on the back of his chair was a sleeping bat. Why didn't he ever pay attention to her, look at her while they were walking down the aisle to their pew? Blessed be the tie that binds; Daddy praying all morning in church that no one will ever make as much money as he does, his bankbook his hymnal.

With the tip of his knife, Curtis speared himself a morsel of crisp fat.

"Crunch is becoming a tyrant." Gina drained her glass and reached for Peter's hand. "He seems so angry all the time, for no reason, out of the blue, jumping on everything Daddy says."

"Forget Crunch, babe, after all it's summer, he's entitled to let off a little steam. And who better than Daddy Maxwell? You don't want Crunch to unload his anger on you!"

"Good Lord, no!"

Peter lay back on the dry grass and reached for Gina's hand. "Tomorrow, he'll be Brother Hug again, I promise."

"Brother Smug," she muttered, fitting herself into the shelter of Peter's shoulder.

"Give me a break, Gina! Can't we enjoy our picnic, can't you live in the now?" She nodded meekly and curled up beside him, her nose pressed into the dry stubble of the summer grass.

Peter set his glass on the ground and inhaled deeply. If only Wendy were here beside him.

Gina moved closer, pressing her body against him. His dear face! She brushed at his cheek with a piece of grass.

He seemed so tense this weekend. She kissed him and lay back, looking at the patterns of leaves against the sky. The two of them were like branches rising from the same tree. And being Gina, she had simple faith that no wind could snap either of them from the tree.

Crunch dumped the bag of groceries on the kitchen table. Wendy put the key to the Zeisses' apartment under the philodendron plant in the hall; Elizabeth hung out in the bathroom, gathering courage for the afternoon's penance.

"You going to drink that whole Coke?" Wendy snapped. Beppo handed her the can. Sometimes she was as disapproving of him as her father was. What a killer, unable to disguise his florid contempt, glaring at Beppo as though he had a condom hanging out of his pocket. Wendy had that same ability to make him feel wrong. He'd never dope out these people. What drove Wendy to dance just out of reach, saying cheerfully, nothing personal, dearie? He wanted to shout, "That's the whole point — it *is* personal."

Crunch wasn't up to the afternoon's crisis. He was mellow with Kate. Saturday afternoon he had been really burned at Peter and Gina for disappearing for the whole day. They hadn't returned to the house until dinnertime. Kate had shrugged it off. "Probably got talking and didn't notice which path they were taking. People get lost in the woods all the time, especially city kids like you and Peter." She'd been right of course.

Kate had a trusting quality. She expected people to be good; she was all up front like Gina. None of the hidden bombs Elizabeth and Wendy buried in their words. While Crunch's mother had rattled around, spewing cliché after cliché about how brave Kate was, how shocking death could be, Kate had remained cordial and polite. And she didn't treat him to any *ratatat* afterward.

It certainly would simplify his life if Elizabeth would accept Kate, and if Wendy didn't look at her as though she were calculating how many miles Kate got to the gallon. Maybe then Kate could become one of them. Beppo had been a success. But today Crunch had to put Elizabeth through as gruelling a questioning as possible. If they weren't vigilant, there wouldn't be a tightknit whole for Kate to join. It was his week, and he wasn't sure he felt up to the test.

Peter felt the imprint of Gina's body as he walked up the hill to his house. They were all probably there already. He resented them for assuming his house was always theirs. He'd convinced Gina to say she had special dance rehearsals three nights a week. His new secret dwarfed the old.

"Come on in, we're having bread and circuses," Crunch called, saluting Peter with a glass of apple juice. They were all eating cheddar cheese and bread Elizabeth had brought.

"Lizzie's providing the refreshment as well as the gore," Beppo said, moving his chair a few inches closer to Wendy's.

"Today begins my week," Crunch began pleasantly. He had to test how much weight the rope would bear before he swung over uncharted territory. "We have no precedent for what Elizabeth did because none of us has ever flagrantly gone against the others."

Wendy bit off a corner of cheese. "First I want to know why the hell she fled with the kid in the dumbest runaway scene since Huck Finn pushed off in the raft with what's his name — Jim."

"Let's not call for the verdict 'til all the evidence is in, *please*." Elizabeth pulled at her braid and looked at each of them in turn. "I was a mess all last week. I slept 'til Friday, you know." No one offered to help her. "So on Saturday morning I decided to face what I'd done." Finally they were listening.

"Done to us!" Wendy said through clenched teeth.

"Done to Dougle." Elizabeth would not be badgered. "So I went to 750 Riverside Drive and had a chat with Worth, N.!"

"Holy Mother of God!" Beppo slid from his chair and drummed his fists on the floor. "You tracked her down? This is better than TV!"

"They live on the seventh floor. The place is proof Dougle lives there. No rugs, no furniture except a card table. His mother races around trying to trap him in the john."

Crunch stretched out on the floor. His shirt worked its way up his body as he twisted in laughter. The louder they laughed the more helpless Wendy felt. Beppo was hitting Elizabeth on the back with the enthusiasm of one dumb jock congratulating another after scoring a touchdown.

Her voice rippling with triumph, Elizabeth took up her story again. She could not resist the temptation to play it broadly. "Their one conventional chair is artistically draped with a shower curtain."

"Does she wear sewer boots?"

"Have they been threatened by the board of health?"

"Was Dougle glad to see you?"

"He's going to a shrink, a *dozen* shrinks," Elizabeth smacked herself on the forehead. "Who else would pick Freud's Frankenstein to save?"

They loved her.

Infuriated, Wendy threw a cushion at Crunch. "Why the hell doesn't somebody open a window? This place stinks of dirty socks."

Nobody stirred.

Elizabeth had reaped more success than she had hoped for. She decided to take a chance. "Anyway I am sorry, genuinely. The whole thing was silly. And thanks to me poor Sam missed the most important siting of the year."

Crunch kicked his legs over his head. "Poor old Sam. He'll have to catch the reruns."

"Not funny," Elizabeth said, tugging on her braid. "It wasn't a caper — I upset people, I involved too many people, not just us. Just plain dumb."

"It's OK, Elizabeth," Beppo told her, putting his arms around her.

"Agree," said Peter.

"Agree," said Crunch.

"You're all repulsive!" Wendy hissed. "She endangered us; she broke our cardinal rule; she lied to us, she kept a secret, she involved outsiders."

"Well it's over and done with," Peter shrugged. "It doesn't seem so important."

"Really!" said Wendy, her face stiff with anger. "And what is more important, Peter? Benny taking snapshots of some Indian tourist trap?"

Peter wished they'd go home. "Wendy, you're carrying on like Lenore when she's caught Benny with a bimbo."

Crunch jumped to his feet. "Let's baptize Wendy in beer, cleanse her of her grouchy old self. Might improve her disposition."

Heat fluttered inside Wendy. They were talking as though *she'd* been wrong, not Elizabeth. How had the power shifted so quickly? In a flash she knew how to get them back. She kicked off her sandals and unbuttoned her shirt. The boys cast furtive looks at one another. Wendy knew the focus would swing back to her.

Conversation stopped. Wendy fell back against the couch as though flung there by the force of Crunch's excited look. His hands were pressed flat against his hips, he rocked back and forth on the balls of his feet. Elizabeth threw Wendy urgent signals, trying to telegraph her fear. She had to break the silence before something terrible happened. "Wendy!" was all she could say, her mouth was too dry to speak. Wendy blew her a kiss. Poor Elizabeth, guys would never pant after anything she could give them.

Elizabeth crossed the room, away from the vortex of terrible energy emanating from the couch. Peter swung his arms wide; chewing her thumb, Elizabeth wondered if there was any way to derail Wendy's power trip. Crunch and Peter stood close to each other. Elizabeth was surprised at how alike they'd grown. Their arms were the same length; their fingers curled against their thighs.

127

Even their jeans had faded to the same hue. She hadn't really looked at them in so long. She turned when she heard Beppo moan softly. He was hugging his arms across his chest, his lips moved, but he uttered no sound. She knew they couldn't push each other much further — but it wasn't she who had the power to stop them.

"All three of you?" Wendy asked, her voice a calypso beat.

Elizabeth's ears roared with the daring of it all.

"Don't look so scared, Beppo," Wendy laughed. "God's sleepin', he ain't watchin' you." Crunch wheeoed and Beppo shook his head as though he had water in his ears.

"They're serious, Wendy," Beppo wailed. "Goddamn it, don't lie there like an open box of candy."

Wendy was starring in the precise caper she had envisioned so often. She was their queen. How could Beppo miss the point so completely! He was as embarrassing as last year's slang. She stared at Crunch until she caught his eye. With the slightest twitch of her eyebrow she caused him to run to the couch and kneel next to her. It had begun.

Elizabeth saw Wendy's body taking on the teasing pose of a magazine ad. She suspected Wendy had practiced this scene. She ran to the couch, put her hand on Crunch's shoulder to restrain him. But before she could speak, Wendy pushed her away, stood up, stripped off her silk shirt and handed Elizabeth her underwear. "Don't look so confused, dearie," Wendy purred.

Elizabeth shuddered at her position — wardrobe mistress. Clutching Wendy's warm underwear she ran from the room. When there had been no noise from the living room for about five minutes, Elizabeth knew she'd have to go back in there, take charge, sort through the mess. Still clutching Wendy's clothes, she stood in the doorway. What she saw froze her to the spot. She tried to act casual, but her attention was centered on the pattern of hair growing straight down from Crunch's belly.

Wendy woke up warm and dry and sleepy. She was not surprised to see Elizabeth standing next to the bed holding out a cup of tea. "Where are the boys?"

"God, Wendy, are you all right?" Elizabeth whispered.

Wendy shifted in the bed.

"Should I call someone, a doctor?" Elizabeth fought the image of herself wiping the moist forehead of a friend dying of yellow fever in an epidemic starring Olivia de Haviland.

"Sure and call the *Times* while you're at it." She closed her eyes. "I'm going back to sleep."

"No! We've got to make sure you're OK."

"It was my caper. I'm calling the shots. Leave me alone."

Elizabeth was ashamed that her hands were trembling. "How could we let it happen? After it was over, Peter and Crunch had to drag Beppo under the shower and hold him under the cold spray. He was carrying on like a wild man. He could have erupted, gotten really *violent,* he's still spooked. Peter was afraid his grandmother might drop over, or that a neighbor would hear Beppo's shouts — we were all panicked!"

Wendy lay with her eyes closed, like Snow White after eating the poisoned apple. Elizabeth touched her cheek.

129

"Do you remember Crunch carrying you in here?"

Wendy showed no more interest than if Elizabeth had been reciting the plot of a TV show.

"It happened, all of it, here, this afternoon."

Elizabeth's high, nervous voice offended Wendy. "I don't want to rerun this. It is over." She did not open her eyes.

Elizabeth touched the sheet that covered Wendy. "What I mean is we have to make sure it never happens again."

"Nothing happened to you!" Wendy said in a dangerously low voice.

"I didn't try to stop it," admitted Elizabeth.

"Did you love every minute of it? Better than all your paranoid suspicions, always insinuating about me, about every boy we ever knew. So you finally got your reward. Did you think they'd want you? Sucker!"

Elizabeth couldn't told back her tears. They burst out of her with such force that she fell forward and wept into the sheet covering Wendy.

"Was it fun to watch?"

"I was sure they'd stop, weren't you? I knew it wouldn't happen, because it couldn't happen." Wendy tried to push Elizabeth's head off her stomach. Elizabeth only cried harder.

"Why are you so hell bent on making me feel guilty?" Wendy asked. The sight of stalwart Elizabeth crying out of control forced her own wrenching sobs. Where had her triumph fled so fast?

Elizabeth looked up and shook her head. "I didn't mean to make you feel guilty," she insisted hoarsely.

"Where are the boys?" Wendy asked through her tears. The sight of Elizabeth sobbing uncontrollably frightened her.

"Crunch and Peter went to put Beppo in a cab. It'll take a lot of bread to find a cab who'll drive him over to Staten Island." Elizabeth tried to sound normal, as though it were an ordinary afternoon. She brought Wendy the pale blue silk shirt and held it while Wendy slipped her arms into the sleeves. "He sure was freaking out, calling for the Blessed Virgin. He came completely unglued."

"You'd think he had witnessed a murder," Wendy said as she buttoned her shirt. Elizabeth felt easier when Wendy's breasts were covered. "Wonder if he'll go to confession?" She smoothed her hair and contained it in her barrette. The worse Beppo behaved, the less Elizabeth would stick out as the oddball.

Wendy grabbed Elizabeth's hands. "If he does go near a priest, I want him cut out like a tumor."

"We can't pretend it didn't happen."

"You can. You were the nonessential one after all."

Elizabeth ran from the room and slammed the door of the apartment. For several blocks she was not aware of store windows, other pedestrians, dogs sniffing knots of garbage at the curb. She smelled no bus exhaust.

A new entity had been forged two hours ago, with Wendy at its center. Elizabeth was a package no one cared to unwrap. Looking up she read the signs in the window of Marty's Meats — chicken breasts, leg of lamb, pork butt, calves liver. The world had become bodies.

8

For a couple of days Elizabeth stayed home. She would not permit herself the comfort of the air conditioner. She lay on the living room couch in a patch of sunlight, arms over her head, inhaling her own sweat. Were they all at Peter's? Was Wendy joking with the boys about her? Unable to stand the thought of what was happening without her, she hurried to the bookstore and charged an armload of books. Back in the silent apartment, she placed the books, spines out, horizontally along the back of her bureau, where they were reflected in the mirror. Were they all at Peter's laughing at her discomfort?

Each day passed bitter as an aspirin caught in her throat. Elizabeth tried not to think about the fact that none of them had called. She bought books and piled them beside her in bed. She selected one with a blue and purple cover. Raising herself on one elbow she flipped through the book, five hundred pages of somebody else's despair.

Five days and no one had called her. She called Crunch and said she had the flu, that was why she hadn't been around. Crunch laughed and said he had hemophilia. She sent Wendy a funny card. She cleaned her closet and arranged her books by subject. She had lunch with Kate at a different restaurant every day, but Kate was a poor substitute. By the end of the week, Elizabeth could sit for almost an hour without seeing the boys bent over Wendy.

Peter knew he was moving much faster than sweet Gina. School was beginning next week. Neither of them would have much free time. Their season was almost at its end. He was outdistancing her.

Yesterday afternoon had told him that — all the time he rubbed his bare foot up and down Wendy's leg, she returning his look of challenge. Crunch had been carrying on about Elizabeth continuing to hide at home. Wendy had edged a few inches closer to Peter and tucked his foot between her thighs. He shifted, she slumped down on her spine. All the while Crunch rattled on about penance and cleaning up the loose ends before school started, Wendy and Peter sat facing each other on the couch, their movements hidden by a large pillow Wendy hugged to her stomach.

"Whatever is eating her, she's got to spit it out," Crunch was still talking. Peter heard his voice and marveled that he could remain so outwardly calm. Even Crunch couldn't guess what was happening.

"We all love Elizabeth," Peter said slowly.

Wendy squeezed her legs around Peter's foot. "She wants to be punished. For all her excuses, she's floundering in banality — she's insisting there's a right and wrong."

"What she doesn't understand is that nothing happened," Crunch said forcefully. Peter felt a spark of embarrassment. Crunch had no sense that he was singing off-key.

"Senior year in high school, the last hurrah, great time, how I envy you." Mr. Maxwell rubbed his hands together.

"Isn't it time to apply to college, dear?" Mrs. Maxwell looked at Crunch as though she couldn't remember something important.

"I'll most likely study deep-sea diving at Coral Reef Tech. It's a school for kids who have fishy excuses for not having the bread for a real education; the profs are mackerel."

Mr. Maxwell did not jump to his son's bait.

Gina sighed and wiped her mouth with her napkin. "Still got the glooms about school? Where's Kate applying?" she added perfunctorily, smiling at her brother to neutralize what might sound like meanness. She suffered more than Crunch when she was nasty to him.

"She's going to work for a year, maybe go to Europe. I gather her folks left plenty of dough, which is to say they didn't run through it, had a clear sense of the future, her folks." He talked against an inner restlessness that kept pulling him toward some explosive action.

Gina pushed her chair back from the table. "I am getting tired of you pulling this crap. Why can't you face up to the fact that we have a family money problem and stop blaming Dad all the time?"

Crunch applauded. "Well said, sister dear. Of course the money problem does not affect your dance classes, Mom's garden, or Dad's gadgets. Just Crunch's life and career plans."

"I can't wait 'til you go away to school. All summer you've been getting meaner and meaner. You're always on my back: Where you going, Gina? Where you been, Gina? And I miss my brother, because you're not Crunch anymore."

"Tough break, Gina. I probably won't be going away to school. I'll probably be lucky to get into one of the city dumping grounds. Remember, there's no money."

"No one is denied a college education these days because they don't have money," Mr. Maxwell took a sip of water and patted his napkin to his lips.

"Sure, we can get the whole town together and put on a show to raise money for Crunch. What do you say, Judge Hardy, can we use your barn?"

"The name Crunch suits you. *Fried corn.*" Gina advanced on him, eyes narrowed, her face flushed. "Nobody's ever had a nail in their shoe except you. Must be great being the only sufferer in the world."

"Don't push me, Gina," he said softly.

"Good night, Mom, Dad," Gina took her plate into the kitchen. They could hear her stacking the dishwasher, but none of them spoke. Mrs. Maxwell took an apple from the fruit bowl, held it a moment, and put it back in the bowl. The front door clicked behind Gina.

Peter ran the last block home. Wendy kept playing quicksilver, promising all afternoon, then suddenly leaving with Crunch. Peter had tried to signal her with his eyes and his hands that he needed her today. Once he was sure of her he wouldn't miss Lenore and Benny, he wouldn't hold on to Gina — if only Wendy would admit to him how great it was, the two of them, alone. Wendy was the sound of one hand clapping! Lenore would understand that. He picked up the phone.

"Sorry I haven't called this week, Lenore, but when I tell you this dynamite thing, you'll understand."

"What time is it, Peter? Benny says clocks bind us to the now."

"Damn it, Lenore, can't we have one normal conversation? I'm tired of having a mother who is a Woody Allen joke."

"You want a Bloomingdale's junkie like Crunch has?"

"Is that the only choice?" He laughed reluctantly.

"Putdowns are cheap, darling. They zap karma."

"Lenore! I'm trying to tell you —"

"Benny's passed into another consciousness."

"Lenore, we both know this is bullshit. Benny's playing Zen just to please you."

"That's how much you know."

His throat ached. He wiped his eyes roughly against his sleeve. "It's all a con," his voice quavered. "Why don't you two come home?"

"I can't understand you. We must have a bad connection. Oh, darling, guess who just emerged from his devotions."

"Boyo, wait 'til you hear! A couple weeks ago we met this tantric holy man. You ought to see this guy, he fasts three months at a time. His ribs look like wires wrapped around his earthly frame. He's tiny, wears the traditional loincloth — nothing like those cheesy ashram locals in orange sannyasi robes panhandling on Fifth Avenue."

"When did you become an expert on holy ready-to-wear?" The words ripped from Peter's throat.

"You know, Peter, there are gurus and there are gurus. Like anything else, you get what you pay for. This guy is connected with the top swamis. They do not come cheap. Anyway he trances and then after a couple of days he comes out to the mesa where I'm meditating, and tells me I'm *clogged,* I need purifying, and he gives me my *mantra.* You wouldn't believe it, kiddo, this swami puts his hands on my head, and the emptiness of unknowing becomes wisdom."

"Can you bear it? Benny is holy," squealed Lenore. "How do you think I feel — all those years I meditated, how many hours of yoga, TM, levitation even, and now it turns out Benny gets the Divine Light."

"I can't keep up this balancing act," Peter screamed through the phone, "pretending to be happy all the time, lucky Peter with so much freedom."

Benny cleared his throat. "You picked a great time to tell us. We're booked on Air India Friday night."

Peter was trembling, his heart was racing. "You're going to India?" he rasped. They had burned up New York and Taos and needed new distractions.

"That's the way it's shaping up." Lenore's voice took on a confidential tone. "Our swami leveled with us. You can't get a top-flight guru in New York. I might have been much further along if I hadn't fallen under the influence of a certain swami, who according to our swami, is notorious for entering people's heads with diabolical intentions."

137

Peter couldn't listen to them another minute. He severed the connection. He sat in the dark, not thinking of much. He decided to sleep on the couch. It seemed like such an effort to take off his clothes and get into bed. He feel asleep next to the telephone, thinking all he had left was Wendy.

Elizabeth held the front door open with her shoulder and thrust her two bulging shopping bags into the hall. As quietly as possible she crept down the hall, the bags knocking against her legs. Once behind the safety of her closed bedroom door, she surveyed her room. There was no place for today's haul. Even her bureau drawers held books; they were stacked under the bed, along the far side of the bed, hidden from the doorway. There were books behind the chair, in piles across the floor of the closet. She had an oversized volume of Blake's poems and a beautifully printed set of his etchings, published in 1889. They were at the bottom of her clothes hamper.

But nameless and formless the fear remained. It abated for a while in the stacks, where she could stretch out in the dark and rest on the cool stone floor of the library, wiping dust from gold-lettered spines. As she fingered the dried-out paper, corners of pages crumbled like fine pastry in her hand. Some volumes had not been checked out in twenty years. It was inconceivable to call the act stealing when no one had thought of the sixth tier since a time before Elizabeth was born.

Her three-inch faculty child ID was all the validation she needed to enter any of the university libraries. She felt exalted each time she slipped a book under her skirt, wedged it between her skin and her underpants. The danger coated her with sweat. The guard barely noticed her. Some days she returned to the top tier and chose more books. Some she smuggled immediately to safety — others she hid behind the refuse cans in the ladies' room. Each day it took a few more books to elicit the hum and rush of excitement, the only feelings which muted the grief choking her.

Hunched over the pile of today's books Elizabeth reminded herself there was one way out of this bone-hard isolation. She fell on the bed, flattening her arms to her sides like a coffin dummy. Staring at the ceiling, she knew she should call Crunch. It was his week and he was the most forgiving. Make the call, Elizabeth, and get rid of the sensation that mildew is creeping up your legs. The words became litany but still she didn't call Crunch. When she went to sleep each night, she hoped she'd wake up the next morning and say "Is that all, no need to carry on so," but she couldn't shake the picture of Wendy and the boys.

She rolled off the bed and began dressing for Tess's stupid Lincoln Center celebration. She knelt on the floor of her closet, her skirt hems touching her forehead. She covered her nose against the sour smell of dirty clothes. Tess exudes roses and I sweat like an animal, she thought. Elizabeth felt tears start in her eyes and wiped them hastily on the rough woolen leg of her gray slacks.

She called out to Kate to ask to borrow pantyhose. Standing in the doorway of the bathroom they shared, Elizabeth watched her cousin, whose back was to her. Dipping her head and manipulating her hair dryer, which looked to Elizabeth like a pink plastic revolver pointed at her head, Kate's movements were as instinctive as a cat washing itself. Elizabeth couldn't manage that highly touted piece of equipment; her wet hair blew across her face and tickled her as it lay plastered to her cheeks. After a few minutes her arm ached from holding the dryer and her eyes stung from the heat. Kate would leave the bathroom a flippy, fluffy triumph of curls.

Kate was familiar with all the gear to service her body. If women were required to be licensed, Elizabeth knew she'd be excluded from the club. Highlights? Hair swept into French twists? She didn't have a chance. Wash it, brush it, braid it.

Back in her room Elizabeth glowered at her reflection in the mirror. She unbraided her hair, poured some cologne onto her hairbrush, and combed her furrowed hair, leisurely, as if she enjoyed it. She lifted her hair off her neck and touched some cologne to her hairline. Even as her flushed face grinned back in the mirror, she knew the feeling of accord with herself would fade, that she would shrink from the unspoken question she heard in the depths of her soul: *Who in this room does not look like a magazine ad?*

Tonight she'd wear one of Kate's flowered prairie skirts.

Tonight she could beat the sense of being a drudge.

Let that be enough, she advised her reflection.

"You feel better this morning, *piccolino?*" Mrs. Santini leaned over Vinnie's pillow and placed her hand on his forehead. "No fever."

"Fever isn't everything, Ma. My muscles ache, my throat is so sore, it seems to be spreading into my ears." He turned away from her look of concern. What a swine he was. She was such an easy mark because her trust bore no taint of suspicion.

"You always had a weak sinus. That's how it starts. When you was little it settled in your chest. Pop says flu is going around." His father had been declaring for years that flu was going around. "You not going to start school tomorrow unless you are completely better." He heard her announce her decision to Pop, which had been Vinnie's intention all along. The back door slammed and his mother was off to Mass. Nothing changed in this house. Beppo kicked off his blankets. He felt gravid with sin. Might as well face it, sin plain sin. That day he hadn't thought sin. He didn't know what he'd thought, if he'd thought. Wendy's splendid rosy body had exploded in his mind, nothing of him had been left — as though he were one of those aliens blasted off the Zaxxon screen. He'd gained Wendy. He'd lost eternal life.

Lying in bed waiting for Berto to finish in the bathroom, Beppo despaired of the odd silence. The void. He felt he should use elegant phrases, Bible words, so long since he'd asked anything of God. He had grown shy. Forgive me, Father, I have violated Wendy. What crap. It had happened so fast. It had been a lark. There had been no thought of sin. God had been waiting for this sin patiently since He was outside time. God quietly waiting with the patience of cats. "Why didn't You stop us?" Beppo cried. He cursed the sound of his tinny words. God's voice came through an echo chamber to the Faithful. Beppo had stopped listening.

Beppo pulled on a T-shirt and jeans. He examined his teeth in the mirror. Santini teeth, long sharp dog teeth. But he was the only killer among them. He swiped at his hair with the comb. He had to get out of the house. He could not hold up under another day of his mother's trusting concern.

Beppo zipped up his jacket and set out for the Boulevard. It had been months since he'd been to the arcade; his old friends had stopped calling, raised their eyebrows when they saw him at Mass, taunting him with their sly looks. But he'd been foolish, selling off all his old connections, thinking the group would be his forever. A few hours in the arcade was just what he needed to forget Peter's apartment, the couch, Wendy.

Angelo and Joyboy were at their usual posts, hunched over the Zaxxon machines, shouting out scores to each other. It seemed like another lifetime when Beppo was proud to see his own name chalked on the giant blackboard over the change booth. He'd hit 442,230 on the Frogger, funny he still remembered it after all this time. He looked to see what the current high-scorers were. "Johnny Richman could never have scored 163,345,220 on the Robotron level three," he said aloud.

"Vinnie, that you? Hey, guys Vinnie Santini's ghost is here!"

"Get bent, Mitchelson. I got better things to do with my time than rack up arcade scores."

"Right, you're the hotshot who goes to school with preppies."

"Say something in Preppie, real Preppie, Vinnie!" Joyboy looked up from his machine. "Better yet, see if you can top me on Zaxxon."

"What about Donkey Kong, that's my meat, rescuing chicks," Vinnie glanced at Joyboy through slitted eyes.

"You ain't seen Donkey *Junior* huh? You been on another planet?"

"Might as well for all the time we seen him," Angelo said, pumping another quarter in Zaxxon.

Beppo went over to the Donkey Kong, Jr. machine and read the screen. Even DK had gone for revenge. Mario has suddenly turned into a louse. The Kong's in jail and gentle Mario is hurling all kinds of deadly birds and evil snapjaws at the trapped beast. Beppo swatted Mitchelson's ass. "I knew it all the time, Mario was the real villain, that's why he's after the Kong. None of you guys ever guessed it was the Kong trying to save the chick from Mario? The one who looks wicked isn't always the wicked one."

Mitchelson shrugged and made a crazy sign in Vinnie's direction. "He's not even in the ballpark no more. Come on, Joyboy, give me a quarter, let me show this zombie how it's done."

Vinnie's score was so low he had to pay a round for each guy. By that time they'd stopped ribbing him about preppies, and they fell into a contest — who could get highest on Ms. Pac-man before lunch. Vinnie tried to play Robotron, but he was so out of practice, those double joysticks were too tough to handle.

"C'mon, Vinnie, we're going to get pizza across the street."

He was grateful that the razzing seemed to have died.

Maybe there was some way he could convince Mom and Pop to let him go back to St. Anne's.

"What's your favorite game, Vinnie?" Angelo asked. "Me, I got this dream someday they'll have like a Three-D game, screens all around me, great sound, with a really tight story, like a movie, not just all this blaster crap. It would be so real you could believe it was happening."

Vinnie tried desperately to think of something cool to respond, to get back in their good graces, but all he could do was nod. "I like your idea, real fine, excellent. I'd like them to make a screen so large you couldn't see anything but the screen, so you'd really think you were there."

The rest of the afternoon went fine. It wasn't 'til he was a block away from home that Vinnie remembered tomorrow was school. Clearly he'd have to cut, buy a little bit more time to get his act together.

It was a piece of cake getting out of the house at seven with his backpack. Ma never even questioned that he was setting off for Demaret. None of the regulars was at the arcade; they had school too. With only a few scruffy guys hanging out there, the machines looked like dead metal aliens. Without the flashing lights and pulsing sounds Vinnie could smell rotting garbage and spilled beer near the door. He felt as though he were alone on the planet.

Around ten o'clock Vinnie hunched his shoulders and set off for the ferry. He could get to Demaret by lunch. He didn't belong with Angelo and Joyboy anymore. Demaret was where he belonged. Wendy was all he wanted. She was the ultimate game.

9

This is the first year since second grade that I've climbed this hill without Wendy, Elizabeth said to herself, on the first morning of school. Senior year, a pile of meaningless razzle without the group. They had infused Elizabeth with the energy to run up that hill to school — Peter on one side, Crunch on the other. Without them she pushed her way up the hill like a weary old woman. "I'll do whatever I have to, whatever she says, to get everything back to where it was," Elizabeth vowed.

"Good morning, sweetheart, welcome to senior year!" Crunch's eyes shone with high spirits. "Tess said you were sick yesterday, but I knew you wouldn't miss opening day assembly."

"Crunch, I need you," Elizabeth raised her voice.

"What? Can't hear you over this din. See you at lunch. And stay out of Wendy's hair, OK?"

The bell rang and the crowd moved toward the stairs. When she reached the landing, Elizabeth turned for an instant and looked at the faces running toward her. There must be a hundred kids on the stairs and none of them knows what happened at Peter's two weeks ago. Elizabeth moved into the narrow space between the rows of students on each side of the staircase, and took the stairs two at a time. She wasn't about to creep along, hugging the banister, giving in to faint-hearted self-pity. "I'm no sleazoid," she reminded herself. "If Wendy says nothing happened, then nothing happened."

Wendy was the first to arrive at the math room. The best senior privilege for them — eating in empty classrooms instead of in the cafeteria. She opened the window and held her face in the cool draft.

"Here's your cottage cheese, madam. And vanilla ice cream. You've been eating an awful lot of pure white food lately." Crunch's dimples belied the possibility of sarcasm. "We'd be operating at full strength today if Beppo were here. Maybe he'll never come back."

"No reason to lend any importance to such foolishness. If he can't take it, he deserves to go back to Staten Island — for the rest of his life, for all I care. As for Elizabeth, it's interesting she can take off with someone's kid and that's morally OK with her. But if we, involving no outsiders, perform one act that shakes her —"

"There's no question of guilt," Crunch said with conviction and turned a chair around to face Wendy.

"Of course there isn't."

"She might have a case if we'd involved an outsider."

Crunch pulled the plastic wrap off his salad and squeezed the envelope of French dressing over the lettuce. "Let's not bring it up if she doesn't. Maybe we can get on with senior year and not *rehash*."

Wendy nodded. "How can you eat that mess? Lettuce like wet paper towels and dressing that tastes like last week's bubble gum." Wendy dipped the tip of her spoon into her cottage cheese.

"I ignore it," Crunch told her with an enormous smile. "I think about something else, and before you know it, it's gone. The Crunch doesn't like something, he makes it disappear."

"Wish you'd make that cafeteria line disappear." Peter held the door open with his shoulder for Elizabeth, who followed him into the room. "The line was about five blocks long. Some clowns from the UN, seeing how typical New York teenagers eat lunch at a ritzy prep school." Peter dragged a chair close to Crunch's. He extended his foot and hooked another chair and dragged it toward himself. He and Crunch stretched their legs across its seat.

Wendy glanced at Elizabeth and giggled. "All I can see are feet."

Elizabeth set her tray on a desk and nodded. Her heart was racing.

"You waiting for an invitation?" Wendy asked coldly.

"Nope, just trying to decide whether to sit on the boy's side or on yours."

"Missed you yesterday, Lizard. Kate and I hoped you'd come with us to the early movie." Crunch patted the chair next to him.

"Must have been at the library," Elizabeth mumbled and set her tray down next to his, across from Wendy.

"Library?" Crunch frowned. "You mean you weren't sick as a hound dog slinkin' out of the rabbit hutch?"

"Crunch, what a dreadful thing to say." Wendy pouted and then laughed uncontrollably.

"Thought I heard the lady laughing." Beppo paused in

147

the doorway, holding his tray at arm's length. He looked around the room. "Just testing the system, to see which program is running. Maybe there's a new configuration."

"Shut up, Beppo," Elizabeth said.

Peter looked at Beppo. "How come you cut this morning?" he asked tonelessly. He hoped it was clear he didn't care about the answer.

Was it only a year ago he'd entered Demaret for the first time? Beppo grinned at Wendy and put his tray next to hers. "Take my ice cream," she said to him. "I'm not hungry."

Beppo continued to grin. He did have a place in the world. Sin was a burned-out star, whose light continued to reach the earth for years after the explosion.

They all sat expressionless, studying their trays. Elizabeth understood that she was meant to stop struggling. "I give up. I want it to be over, I want us to be the way we were."

"You sure?" Wendy spun a pencil on the desk.

"I'm willing to live by the new rules." Further than that she would not sink. She hoped her tone of voice made that clear.

"Well spoken, third duck." Wendy said softly.

"What in hell is the third duck?" Peter asked.

"Don't you know how ducks make it?" Wendy raised her eyebrows and leaned forward in her chair. She put her dish of cottage cheese on the desk behind her and looked around the circle. Elizabeth dug her nails into her palm. How could she have thought time was on her side?

148

"First, ducks do it in the water. So the male duck —"

"The drake," Peter interrupted.

"This is my story," Wendy told him, "unless you think you can improve on it." She had warned him to expect no special treatment. Last night she would not allow him to touch her once they'd got dressed. When she turned from the mirror in his parents' bedroom and dropped the hairbrush into her bag, he had been holding a small shiny object in his palm. She took it from him, slipped it into the pocket of her jeans, and chuckled. "Thanks for the key, Peter," she said, irony all over her face. "But remember, it fits your lock, not mine." His head had lolled forward the way it did when he had been smoking good dope. "Whatever you want, whenever you say," he'd said. Then his voice quit on him.

"Hey, Wendy, I got to know about the little ducks, lunch period is ticking away," Crunch said, pointing to the clock on the wall.

"You'll be the delight of the Banker's Club, keeping the program moving," Wendy answered, exultant. She held all their keys. "So, anyway, the male duck grabs the female at the back of the neck." She put her cupped left hand over her right. "And he bites her like this. *Hard!* Her head dips down, quite a ways under the water, forcing her rear into the air. Then the males sticks his —" she stiffened the middle finger. "All the while a third duck is treading water, boys, watching, just a few feet away from the action."

"At least the third duck won't drown," Elizabeth said in a silky tone.

"Well, that's the show for today, folks," Crunch laughed nervously.

Peter felt his heart ready to burst out of his chest. "What if they can't find a third duck?"

"There's always a third duck," Wendy said handing him her knapsack. "Drop my books in the art room, Peter."

A month later Elizabeth had acquired fifty more books. Late at night she lay on the floor and slipped out several volumes from under the bed or behind the desk. Reading the books was the only time she felt free of the sense of betrayal. The boys lapped around Wendy; Beppo had lost his timidity. He was reckless, kissing Wendy's shoulder when he passed her in the corridor, whispering in her ear at lunch, feeding her vanilla ice cream from his spoon. All the while Elizabeth waited in dread for more third-duck fables. She filled the void with books.

One afternoon crossing Broadway Elizabeth saw three old women sitting in a patch of sunlight on upturned orange crates in front of the supermarket. One of them looked over her shoulder each time the exit door hissed open. Any minute the manager might order them off his crates. Elizabeth could not ignore such an arcane message. If she could not adapt to the new rules she would be propelled into a world lacking even a semblance of grace. A world in which she would be grateful for a couple of hours in the sun, breathing the worn air of Broadway.

Elizabeth suspected some powerful alliance was building between Wendy and Peter. She had to try one final time to confront Wendy. They no longer rotated weeks. It always seemed to be Wendy's week. If they were to get back to what they had had before August, then Elizabeth had to make Wendy see that she'd taken the power, and it was leading them to ruin. She had to take the risk. As things stood the boys were gaily painted carousel horses moving up and down separate poles to Wendy's tune, one that caused Elizabeth to stumble.

It started out well enough. Elizabeth was sitting in her chair and Wendy was sprawled across Elizabeth's bed, just like any late fall day since they were both small enough to sprawl across the bed.

"Didn't you adore Crunch storming around because his ammonia gases weren't accurate?" Wendy waved her arms lazily. "So much for the homilies about males having a natural bent toward science."

"So much for any homilies. They're getting smashed daily."

"Remember the summer we were fighting our parents not to send us to separate camps —"

"No, I do not remember." Elizabeth did not want the conversation to fly off into memory.

"Sure you do, after fifth grade. You were earth, I was fire, Peter water, and Crunch air. We carried candles and chanted!"

Ordinarily Elizabeth enjoyed proof of their closeness. "It's not natural, Wendy" — she plunged in head first — "for us to block what happened, and what's still happening."

Wendy sat up straight. "I won't listen to your innuendoes, and the boys support me a hundred percent." The water was colder than Elizabeth had thought.

"We have to deal with it. Maybe it'll even make us closer."

"Clean up your act, Dr. Feelgood."

Elizabeth blocked the door. "I don't know what to do."

"Don't worry. You're not pregnant."

"What's the next caper, if we insist nothing happened? We could murder a person and shrug it off."

"Got anybody in mind?"

"I see Peter looking at you his face all fuzzy, and Beppo feeding you candy mints. Things are different, admit it!"

Wendy's wintry eyes caused Elizabeth to shiver. "Tired of being the third duck?"

"If you were sleeping with a guy you were involved with, I mean if you had a beau —"

"A beau! And now a word from Henry James!"

"Making me feel clunky won't resolve it."

"You're worried about one thing — to hell with all your sanctimonious preaching. You're afraid we're going to leave you out."

Elizabeth's head felt heavy with hot tears. "Maybe that's true."

Wendy was unnerved by Elizabeth's broken sobs. "Christ, Elizabeth, run this morality hype on Kate. Why accuse me, blame me — don't you love me anymore?"

Elizabeth looked up, surprised by the change in Wendy. "Even that day we got the silver punch bowl and cups from Tiffany's, I felt there was a fence around each of our capers, and that we all knew the fence was there. This

152

time we're in the dark, running unchecked — in a universe that knows no bounds."

Suddenly cold, Wendy wrapped her coat around her shoulders. There was something too terrifying about Elizabeth's vision. "It's not like that," Wendy said fiercely, more to comfort herself than to help Elizabeth.

"I need to know there's something containing us." Elizabeth clenched her hands in frustration. "I don't know any other way to say it. It's as though the earth were flat and we were coming dangerously close to falling off without even knowing we're at the edge."

"Of course there's no fence, keeping us like cows in a pasture. You run until you're tired. Open your eyes, Lizard. People are sitting all over a fenceless field, each involved in his own business, like a million separate picnics going on at once."

"I need a fence," Elizabeth said softly.

Wendy knotted her silk scarf around her neck and moved toward the door. "There are no fences except where we choose to build them." She hugged Elizabeth's stiff unyielding body. "You're right about one thing. We should get back on track. Next week will be Peter's, then Crunch's, then yours. See, three fences just put up, OK?" She hugged Elizabeth until she could feel her shoulders relax.

"I knew all we needed was to talk."

After Wendy left, Elizabeth sat on her bed, wondering if Wendy would always have the power to make her feel foolish.

"Can I come in?"

"Sure, Sam." Elizabeth's face brightened. "Just the person I need to talk to. Sam, tell me, if you thought your friends were making a serious mistake —"

"Poor Lizzie, you know enough to follow your own counsel."

"I don't know anything, Sam. Maybe if I were a scientist, I could know something. Then I'd feel *filled!*"

He held her in his arms clumsily. She was as big as he was. "I can track a star, but I cannot direct its progress."

"Some days I wish I'd get sucked up by a black hole."

He laughed. "We all feel that way. But remember, dear, we only postulate that black holes suck up creation. It's the gravitational force from a mass that large that makes the star collapse." He was teaching his way out of that raw moment. He feared black holes less than a weepy daughter. When had either he or Tess ever heard what she said?

Sam was gazing at the ceiling, as though it were the evening sky. "A century ago we thought we were snug at the center of the universe. Galaxy meant immensity. Now we know there are thousands of millions of galaxies."

Elizabeth frowned sharply to remind him that he had asked what was troubling her?

"But of course we don't know the average density of space." He got up, took a piece of paper from his desk and uncapped his pen. "There's a postulated formula for the average density —"

Elizabeth plucked her father's sleeve. "Please disconnect the lecture. I don't care about the density of space."

"You and my students," he answered cheerfully.

She kissed his cheek and gently nudged him toward the door. Defeated she sat down on the bed. Maybe Wendy was right. The only boundaries were ones they made for themselves. As she surveyed the books in stacks behind the bed, she struggled against what she knew. Tomorrow she'd better start taking those books back to the libraries where they belonged. They couldn't protect her any more than Sam could.

10

I've got to stay in town this weekend, Mom. All-day rehearsals Saturday and Sunday." Gina poured gravy on her meat, her hand steady. Her lies had the surety of truth. "The Christmas show is only a month away." She passed the gravy boat to her father.

"How dreary, honey. So many rehearsals. I know it's important to you, but rehearsing so much for a show that only runs two weekends?"

"That's show biz, Mom," Gina flashed a, smile.

"If they got it right the first time, they wouldn't have to rehearse." Crunch leered at his sister. "They never have rehearsals at Demaret. We decide on a play and step onto the stage the same night."

"Stop twitting your sister," Mr. Maxwell said in a tired tone.

"As long as we have extra room, why not invite Elizabeth?" Mrs. Maxwell leaned toward her son. "She hasn't been up all fall."

"I suppose so," he replied. "She's so hard on Kate, it makes it awkward —"

"What about Wendy?" Gina bit her lip. She'd almost

156

said "since Peter won't be coming." But Crunch wouldn't know that 'til tomorrow morning. She'd have to be careful, so many times in the last week she'd almost slipped.

"It's lovely the Maxwells have room for both you girls this weekend." Tess opened her briefcase and took out a blue file folder.

"Crunch has been saying for weeks that Elizabeth should come, but she's always rushing off to the library."

Elizabeth looked at Kate, willing her to be silent, glaring as evilly as she dared under Tess's scrutiny.

"I'm glad you're coming." Kate smiled at Elizabeth's angry face. She wished she didn't sound so bush.

Elizabeth cringed. There was no reason for Kate to be glad. It was an impossible time of year. The brittle meadow grasses were burned brown, stooped toward the frozen ground. Even the branches of the trees were wire-thin frizzle against the grim November sky. None of it was shelter for Kate and Crunch. They would not be glad Elizabeth was there, a lidless eye who couldn't blink to afford them a moment's privacy.

The whole world was breaking into pairs.

"Has there been some problem between you and Crunch?" Tess asked.

"Crunch and I are connected for life, depend on it."

Retreating to her room, Elizabeth dragged out her duffel bag and hastily stuffed it with two heavy sweaters, their arms entangled. She squatted next to the bed and selected a couple of books from behind the nightstand. She wrapped them in a flannel nightgown.

Yesterday afternoon Wendy had presented Peter with

a pair of jeans on which she had appliquéd a red heart. High on the left thigh next to the crotch. Elizabeth heard Wendy laughing in a foreign language. She mumbled what was becoming her daily exit line, "Yadada library, yamamama tomorrow."

"Can I come in?" Kate stood in the doorway, hesitating, as though expecting a blow.

"Of course." Elizabeth wished she could be nicer to Kate.

"A girl in my chem class gave me two tickets to the concert at Carnegie Hall tonight. I was hoping you'd come with me," Kate said, pretending not to notice Elizabeth's disheveled hair, flushed face. What could she be doing squatting over all those books?

"Take Crunch. I have work to do." How many of the books had Kate seen? Would she recognize that they were from the college library?

"I'd rather go with you. You know so much about music. But if you'd prefer, we could go out to dinner. Tess and Sam are going out. We could go to the two-blocks-down Chinese."

"Or the two-blocks-up Chinese. Sure, let's do it," Elizabeth said. Might as well be irritated at a bird for flying as at Kate for glowing.

"Maybe we'd better finesse the concert. I have three chem assignments to write up for my tutor."

"Crunch can't help you there. I've never known him to be baffled the way he is in chem lab."

Kate laughed and went back to her room for her coat. Elizabeth tossed her knapsack over her shoulder and waited for Kate in the hall. Suppose they decided to include Kate as one of them without even asking Elizabeth? She'd been expecting something of the sort ever since Kate socked her with the shovel on the beach. Maybe it was time to cross that off Kate's permanent record. Elizabeth scowled at her reflection in the hall mirror. "Let me borrow your lipstick," she said as Kate came swinging down the hallway.

After dinner, swelled with a strong sense of her new resolve, Elizabeth dialed Wendy. "I've decided to go to the Maxwell's widlife preserve after all. It's easier to go, otherwise I have to listen to Tess reminisce about the golden days of her popular youth." As she said it, Elizabeth recoiled. She couldn't remember Tess ever doing such a thing. She hurried on. "Peter will probably come. It won't be me and them."

"Wrong! Peter's staying in town. Something about painting his grandmother's kitchen cabinets."

"Why don't you come then?"

"Beppo will chew through his web of Mama Spaghettini and we'll go to a museum or something. I think you're nuts to go through three hours in the car, Crunch sniping at Mrs. Maxwell every time she opens her gold-plated mouth. He's even telling Gina to drop dead lately. Remember when Gina was the sun and moon to him?"

"Maybe that's why she's staying in town."

"So it'll be just you and Kate and Crunch. Sounds swell."

"Not as though it's a new act," Elizabeth said drily.

"Last time I went up, Mrs. M told Kate about this

friend of hers who'd contacted her drowned son on the *other side.* Maybe this medium could help Kate contact her parents, *wheeeooo!"*

Elizabeth groaned. "Mrs. Maxwell's on the other side and doesn't even know it."

"Stay home, Elizabeth."

"Is that an order?"

"We could do a movie marathon. You pick the movies!"

Elizabeth was surprised at Wendy's insistence on her company. "I would rather shovel out the monkey cages at the zoo than go to Rockland, but Kate's been miserable, and I'm the reason. I've declared this Be Nice to KC Month, starting today."

"You can't help her parents dying. You always do that, putting yourself between the person and the sun. We cast our own shadows."

She wants me to depend only on her, Elizabeth thought.

Peter lay in bed touching the tips of Gina's hair. The bright morning sunlight had awakened him. He slipped his hand under Gina's nose to feel her warm breath. As he watched the sheet rise and fall, its folds changed Gina back into the little kid he'd known many years ago. He recognized that this time had been their last. She was too soft, too quiet. Wendy was sudden, endless as the New Mexico sky.

Wendy kept bumping into people. When she wanted scrambled eggs, her mother was frying eggs. Her father was listening to his Mantovani records; she was sickened by the saccharin the old goat unleashed at top volume,

160

calling it music. She wandered into her bathroom and took off her nightgown. Studying her body in the mirrors surrounding the tub, she breathed deeply and locked the door. A few minutes later she dressed quickly and set off for Peter's apartment.

"Why can't it keep 'til Monday?" Elizabeth pleaded. She tried to muffle the receiver against her shoulder. Wendy was screaming, and Mrs. Maxwell was peeling carrots a few feet away.

"It's your week, Elizabeth. If you and Crunch aren't back here tonight, we are finished."

"As you said, it's my week," Elizabeth turned away from Mrs. Maxwell. "And I say we wait 'til Monday."

"No, it's got to be now." Wendy's voice deteriorated into sobs.

"Can't you tell me on the phone what's making you so crazy?" Elizabeth could conceive of no disaster that could destroy them. So much of their solidarity was built upon confounding danger.

"He has defiled us."

"*Who?* Beppo?" Who else could it be?

"Be on the next bus."

Elizabeth smothered the phone against her sleeve. Wendy hung up, but Elizabeth chatted on to lead Mrs. Maxwell away from the scent. "OK, we'll try to come back. Of course we want to help your mom." Smiling blandly at Mrs. Maxwell, Elizabeth hung up the phone. "Wendy's mother has a dinner party, and her caterer just went bankrupt, or so he says. Anyway she needs me to help on dish detail and Crunch to be the bartender."

161

Without waiting for an answer, Elizabeth tiptoed back to the living room. Crunch and Kate were reading. "Crunch, I need you in the kitchen."

"Ask Mom. She's better in the kitchen than I am," he replied.

"Crunch," Elizabeth snapped, *"Stonehenge."*

Crunch threw his book across the room. "Have you lost your mind?" He followed her outside to the deck.

Through the window Kate watched Elizabeth talking and Crunch beating his fists in the air. Elizabeth ticked one, two, three on her fingers. Crunch nodded. They stared at each other. Elizabeth began talking again, very rapidly, nervously twirling her braid. Crunch inclined his head to her mouth, a frown on his face.

Only a pane of glass separated them from Kate, but their accord multiplied the distance a hundred times. Kate didn't understand any of it. Whatever it was, they were probably complicating the situation needlessly, the way they had the night Elizabeth had taken Dougle.

Elizabeth shouted into Crunch's face, "We have to go!"

Crunch socked the railing and yelled, "What the hell is this all about?" Kate could hear his outrage quite plain through the glass. More of their secrets she knew nothing about. She fell face down on the couch, unnerved by a look on Crunch's face she'd never seen.

"Katy Callahan." Crunch tapped lightly on her shoulder.

Knock on some other door, she wanted to shout, but Kate had never been one to rage and carry on like Elizabeth and Wendy.

"Kate, my angel, we have a distressing situation." She

bet from his tone that his rubber face reflected none of the menace she'd seen so plainly a moment ago.

"Elizabeth and I have to go home. Something about helping Wendy's mother. Oh, I hate to leave you, but it can't be helped." He leaned over to kiss her just as she was raising her head from the couch. Her skull cracked him sharply on the nose. "Kate, be reasonable," he said, feigning great pain.

"I don't go to Demaret, I don't have to do whatever you say."

"You are *cross*. Take a long walk in the woods, you'll be restored in no time."

"I don't want to be restored. I'm tired of being shut out."

Elizabeth stood in the doorway, her chin resting on her knuckles. Crunch chewed his lips, a frown appeared and disappeared, finally he looked directly at Kate and smiled. "You know what we'll do, lass? We'll go to dinner some place swank this week, we'll wear evening clothes and *flow* downtown on my old man's solution to dwindling funds — plastic."

"*No more,*" Kate shrieked. Startled, Crunch backed away. "No more words! All of you bury everything important in mounds of words." Kate dipped her head and rubbed her eyes on her sleeve. Elizabeth rushed to her.

She felt clumsy, sitting on the couch holding Kate, but she didn't let go. Kate turned to Crunch, her body resting against Elizabeth. "I'm not supposed to talk about my parents because Crunch has no material on death. I'm not supposed to notice how you all speak a secret language in front of outsiders like me."

163

Elizabeth knelt still holding Kate loosely. "I've been so awful to you."

Both girls were crying. Dismayed Crunch shoved his wristwatch under Elizabeth's nose. "We have to run, or we'll miss the bus."

"Come home with us, KC, our meeting won't take long."

"I hate being the bad news. We have to leave *now*." Crunch blew Kate a kiss.

"We do have to go," Elizabeth agreed reluctantly. She hugged Kate fiercely. As a down payment.

"How could you let her say those vicious things? Why didn't you tell her to leave? And how come she has a key?" Gina screamed. She was standing over Peter, who lay on his back, still naked, too dazed to move.

"She called me a tramp, and all you did was mumble."

Peter wished Gina would leave before Wendy came back.

"What were you waiting for? Crunch to ride to your rescue? What's her hold over you?"

Gina looked as stiff as the paper flowers Lenore collected in Taos. Perhaps if he flattered her, she would leave without any more fuss. "I love your hair," he said, enunciating each word precisely. He needed sleep. Maybe when he woke up again, the sun would be back in the sky instead of taking up the whole damn bedroom.

"I never realized Wendy was in charge," Gina glowered at him. "I always thought Crunch ruled the roost."

Peter yawned and ran his hand over his chest. "She's probably telling Crunch right this minute."

164

"Who cares! What we've got is normal. *She's* the looney tunes!"

"The penance, the penance," Peter whispered. He covered his eyes, that sun was coming nearer, as if it meant to swallow him.

"You don't care about me." Gina sobbed.

"It might be a good idea if you went home, give us both a chance to get our heads together."

"I'm going home all right, I'm going to soak in a hot bath, for the first time, today, I feel dirty." Her voice broke. Her face was turned away from him but her pain was clear.

"We'll talk tomorrow."

Gina's voice was barely audible. "Was there ever a time when you would have protected me?"

"What gives, what has Wendy so up-ended?"

Peter didn't reply. He led Crunch and Elizabeth into the living room. He sat across the room from them, in a wing chair, his legs pulled up, his feet on the chair. There had been no time to shower. The bedroom was a mess. He had considered beating it out of there, flying to Taos before any of them showed up. But then he remembered, Lenore and Benny were in India.

"Wendy came over about noon. I had given her a key so I didn't hear —"

"When did you give her a key?" Crunch asked. "I had to leave the country and bounce around on a bus because you gave Wendy a key! Did you know about this, Lizard?"

"Not a bit of it."

"What other secrets have you and Wendy been hatching?"

"When she got here, I wasn't — expecting her." They looked at him expectantly. "I was not dressed."

"Caught you in the buff? Now it gets better!" Crunch chortled.

"Something is missing from your account. Wendy wouldn't bottom out because she saw Peter naked. Again." Elizabeth felt removed from the tragedy if indeed there was one. Peter's dark eyes looked like holes, he was sitting so still, waiting for judgment. He had none of the righteousness she had felt the night she ran off with Dougle. His face was chalky white. Not the best moment to remind him she had seen him naked too.

"You telling us the whole number, exactly as it went down?" Crunch's foot beat an uneven rhythm on the floor.

Peter leaned forward. "No. I am truly sorry. It was a mistake, it got away from me, I never thought you'd find out. This was going to be the last time. Even before Wendy —"

"What are you talking about?" Elizabeth asked crisply.

Peter hung his head.

Crunch's face lit up. "A lady! You were getting it on when Wendy arrived! Don't worry, old bean. I'll confess too. Last summer while you guys were all away —"

Peter slid to the floor. Crouched with his arms over his head as though expecting a violent blow, he raised his head a few inches and looked at Crunch. "Gina! It was Gina."

Crunch's foot jerked up toward Peter's face, but Elizabeth caught it in time. Crunch growled inaudibly. Elizabeth went to him, stroked his head. He collapsed against her stomach and rubbed his face back and forth against her sweater. She hoped she could steer them away from disaster.

"Ask him how long, how many times?" Crunch mumbled.

"We can't let this destroy us, Crunch." Elizabeth hadn't a clue how to solve this one. Peter had been asking for trouble messing with Gina. The doorbell rang. Elizabeth half-lifted Crunch. Arms around each other they limped to the door.

Beppo grinned uncertainly. "Was it what Wendy said? Gina and Peter in bed, very naked, industrial-strength top job, et cetera!"

Crunch broke from Elizabeth and hurled himself on Beppo. "You guinea bastard, don't you dare talk about my sister that way." He clutched the collar of Beppo's shirt and ripped the shirt right down the middle.

Elizabeth was timid in the face of so much unpredictable behavior. "Crunch! You can't do this. You've got to cool down."

His hands shot up in the air, as though in surrender. "She's my sister." He spun in a circle. "Peter ruined my sister."

Peter gradually moved closer to Crunch, emphasizing his caution. "It was not dirty, the way Beppo implied. It was love, we were going to tell you soon."

Crunch's face was red as a steak. Elizabeth knew she had to move him and Peter apart. They had grown massive to her. She was afraid one of them would erupt.

"I loved her and she loved me," Peter whined.

"Last week you loved us," Elizabeth told him.

A blow was struck on the outside door. Beppo stretched out his arm to open it. He had an eager look on his face, as though he were about to win whatever was behind the door. But Elizabeth knew better.

Wendy stood framed in the doorway. Elizabeth took her hand from Crunch's arm. Peter braced himself inwardly, but gave no outward sign of his terror. Beppo held the door and gazed into her face, but Wendy looked through him, as though he were one of the door's hinges.

Everything depends on how well she controls the first critical minutes. Without a word Wendy walks to the living room, the group following close behind. When she turns to face them, she is calm.

"Well, Peter, what did you do with your honey, put her in the freezer 'til later, so you wouldn't have to share her?"

"She went home," Peter's tone is polite.

"She was my sister," Crunch cries.

Beppo sits next to Wendy. He wishes he had the guts to put his arm around her. "Peter's been humping, huh," he offers instead.

"He ruined her." Crunch thumps the couch with a pillow. "She was only a kid."

"What else have you kept from me?" Wendy asks evenly.

"You were banking that no one would find out." Elizabeth is trying to telegraph to Peter that he's not alone, there's a rational way out of this.

"No one had so far," Peter replies gamely.

"Gina and Peter have been laughing at me behind my

back, all these months, she's been running me down, they've been getting it on in the country, all those walks, pretending to be lost in the woods, I'll show them who gets the last laugh, at least Peter had the guts to stay here and face the music." Crunch can't make sense of the thing, but he's grateful to Wendy for being so angry on his behalf. What are friends for?

"Where did she go, Peter?" Crunch asks casually, a plan beginning to take shape.

"What's the penance?" Beppo glances around the room. In his neighborhood Crunch would have been at Peter's throat by now. The fight would last until a couple guys separated them and Peter would stay out of sight for a few days. But this was Manhattan, where words were thicker than blood.

Crunch can not recall Gina's face, only her sarcastic voice, running him down at dinner. "She's been doing it with my best friend," he whispers.

"Well, I suppose I've seen the last of Gina," Peter says tentatively.

"You suppose!" Crunch rises from the couch but Wendy pushes him down again. He glares at Peter wordlessly.

"The problem is far more complex than Peter and Gina. Peter betrayed us. Our trust." Wendy inhales deeply.

"That's right, now I see," Crunch says excitedly.

"He did his damnedest to destroy us," Wendy reminds them.

"There shall be no other lady before me," Elizabeth whispers. How could Peter hope to slake Wendy's thirst

169

for revenge? "Would you mind so much, Crunch, if it hadn't been Peter?" Elizabeth wonders aloud.

"It was Peter."

"If Peter swears never to see Gina again?" Beppo suggests.

"What does that do to restore *us?*" Wendy snaps. "No amount of wishing we could turn back time is going to erase what Peter has done." Wendy knows she will win, but she's not yet certain what prize will ground this unspeakable buzzing, like an electric current gone wild, sparking every ounce of her. She settles back on the couch. It's time to bring Elizabeth into it. "It's your week. You call the tune."

"Me? I don't know. I do think no more Gina in Peter's life, in his bed, is necessary, but probably not sufficient." It was hard to imagine Peter conducting a full-fledged secret affair with little Gina Maxwell, who used to lose her mittens three times a week.

They work the same ground over and over. For Crunch Gina is fading now, as though he hasn't seen her in years.

Beppo wants to be the star. "We have so many unknowns. Let *x* stand for Peter. If we only had the computer here."

"Nothing's unknown, we know too much," Elizabeth says. Beppo's earnestness is so transparent to her. These days he makes love to Wendy from every sentence.

Wendy smiles, her body is finally cooling, she no longer feels walled in by their voices. "What is required, Peter, is the opposite but equal action. A force born of as much passion as that charming scene this morning —"

Crunch has been pacing. "She's getting away with it,

she lied to me, all those phony rehearsals, conniving little bitch pretending to be Daddy's gumdrop. I could kill her."

Wendy hugs Crunch. "Peter might prefer her to us." She's got the wind at her back.

"Never! I didn't think she was a threat. I took her like we swiped the punch bowl."

"What Peter did came too soon. Somebody was bound to take up with an outsider. What about Crunch and KC?" Elizabeth is desperately trying to sort through the mess.

"I'd never score KC!" Crunch appeals to Wendy.

"Afraid to make a decision, Elizabeth?" Wendy's runing free, home toward port.

"I'm not afraid of a decision. What does frighten me is how you want to fan the flames instead of quenching them. We have to devise new rules so we can survive this. Peter had a fling —"

"You call screwing my sister a *fling?*"

Wendy strokes Crunch's hand, then brushes her fingertips across his palm.

"Elizabeth's long suit has never been physical, if you follow me. Lord knows who else Gina is playing around with, after all she has the run of the city, she's got your folks conned, even you were fooled, Crunch. She's polluted all of us."

Elizabeth is growing alarmed. The boys are listening raptly to Wendy. Crunch snaps his fingers under her nose. She looks at him blankly. He and Peter are two toy giants, their movements at the mercy of batteries, they are drawing their energy from Wendy. She glances at Beppo, a high-strung terrier barking when his mistress is nearby.

And what of herself? Spinning straw all the time and calling it gold. On her way to scuttling Gina as thoughtlessly as she had Dougle and Kate.

Crunch shakes Elizabeth by the shoulder. "Let me make the decision easier for you. I have no sister. I have no family."

"We are family," Elizabeth tells him and squeezes his hand. "We all know you're sitting on the edge of a knife. This must be awful for you." A pallor Elizabeth has never seen on Wendy's face padlocks Elizabeth's mouth.

Wendy is losing patience with Elizabeth. "Gina must pay."

"She must be punished. Severely," Beppo says, thrilling to the words.

"Come off it. Can't you just picture little Gina seducing Peter? According to Wendy the kid's become Eve, dazzling a helpless Adam, until he forgets the Great Warning." Elizabeth ignores the groans around her. "Gina's the powerless one. Some Eve, some evil."

"I didn't seduce her, she was all over me, said she loved me from the third grade," Peter bellows and sits next to Beppo on the couch, next to Wendy.

"Elizabeth must be excused, Peter. She doesn't know how these things work. Remember this is the same Elizabeth who quivered so stupidly, who was desperate to suffer martyrdom, because of one afternoon's caper, right here on this couch." Wendy smiles into Peter's eyes. "Peter is willing to accept his penance, and I for one respect him for it."

"You don't expect us to buy this crapola?" Elizabeth asks, but none of them is paying any attention to her. She

172

fights the image of the third duck. She has to get through to them. "Let's find Gina —"

"Now you're talking sense," Wendy licks her lips.

"She might be at a movie or on her way to some other guy, one of those dancers who're always *partnering* her." Crunch sneers. "We'd better try the subway station."

"That's not what I meant,' Elizabeth sighs. She feels as though she's sitting in waist-high taffy.

Peter grabs Crunch's hand. "We don't have much time. Set the caper, Elizabeth. We are in this together, all of us. I see that now, we'll wipe the slate clean." All their anger had been beating against Peter like rain against a window-pane. He felt relieved to be one of them again.

Elizabeth is weary. They sound like kids trying to impress each other. Hollow talk.

Crunch is grinning. He rakes his hand through his hair. "I should have known we'd recognize what has to be done. We have only one choice."

Peter rakes his hand through his hair. "We must sacrifice whatever threatens us."

"Five as one," Wendy pushes Peter and Crunch together. She raises her arms and embraces Crunch lightly. Then she steps back and embraces Peter.

"Give me a turn," Beppo dances around the perimeter.

Elizabeth scowls and pulls on her coat. "Any minute Joan Crawford is going to burst wild-eyed from the closet. C'mon, Beppo, I'll walk you to the train, it's getting late."

"Who the hell are you to mock us?" Wendy feels the intoxicating heat of what they are about to do. "Nobody stands in our way."

"*Your* way." Elizabeth answers mildly. "It's growing

173

repetitive. We came home from the country, left Kate alone, subjected Peter to the rack, tested his loyalty, now what do you say we call it a score and get ice cream cones?"

None of them answered her.

"What has been the point to all our capers if not the ultimate!" Wendy says exultantly.

Crunch sees the whole situation now. It's been Gina all along — making him look unimportant, not worth the old man's time. "She might be at the Aphrodite, having coffee. She goes there after rehearsal. It's a couple minutes from here."

Beppo rushes after Crunch. "Wait for me, I'm in this as much as anybody."

"Goddamn old biddies upstairs swapping lima bean recipes," Crunch drawls as he leans on the elevator button.

The boys laugh. They are knotted together.

As they move apart, the elevator door opens. Wendy holds her hands out to the boys. She presses her hands against her hot cheeks and turns back into the apartment to wait for them to return. It will require superhuman effort to forgive Elizabeth.

Elizabeth is still in the kitchen, drinking a glass of water. Wendy leans against the sink. "You'd better wait for the boys since it is still your week. If you walk out of here, it is forever, final, no changing your mind." The words pass through Wendy like an electric current.

Elizabeth reaches for her knapsack, lumpy with books about mosses and ferns for her country weekend, and swings it high into the air. "Frankly, my dear, I don't give a damn."

174

The slamming door echoes in the hall. Trembling, Elizabeth punches the elevator button and catches sight of the five stones she had etched the night she fled with Dougle. She is tired of messing up people's lives. They have left Kate weeping in the country. Now the boys, set in motion by Wendy, running some crazed derby of righteousness, are going to wound Gina until she too will be left weeping and feeling shabby. Or worse.

All for Wendy. Wendy testing her boys. The elevator opens and Elizabeth jabs *lobby*. Heart pounding, she runs through the lobby, her knapsack slapping against her back.

A strong wind impedes her progress up the hill. She thrusts her head forward and fights the force of the wind. "They don't intend to stop this time. They're not going to be satisfied with humiliating Gina."

Picking up speed, Elizabeth scans doorways. Prove me wrong, please prove me wrong. More than anything, she's hoping to find Crunch leering triumphantly. "Just a one-act caper, old Lizard, to show you how pious you've become." More than anything Elizabeth wants to hear them tell her "It would never have come to that. It was all a game."

But she sees no one she knows.

She stops at the curb and looks over her shoulder. Please God, don't let me be too late.

Wendy is nowhere in sight. The boys have several minutes headstart. Elizabeth changes direction. She'll have to run if she's going to catch them, absorb their anger in time.

Across Broadway the sign flashes *Don't walk.*

"The hell you say," Elizabeth mutters under her breath.

She holds up her hand and zigzags through the cars and yellow cabs, waving at their angry horns.

She pauses for an instant on the other side of the avenue. Her knapsack is slowing her down. She slips it off her shoulders and throws it into the trashcan. Books and all.

"I've still got time," she shouts into the wind. "Come on, Elizabeth, make a run for it."